Enjoy!

Jane D. Strickler

MORE THAN SHE BARGAINED FOR

Jane Vinson Strickland

WESTBOW
P R E S S®
A DIVISION OF THOMAS NELSON
& ZONDERVAN

NIV -Scripture quotations are taken from the Holy Bible, New International
Version®, NIV®. Copyright © 1973, 1978, 1984, 2011 by Biblica, Inc.™
Used by permission of Zondervan. All rights reserved worldwide.

WestBow Press books may be ordered through booksellers or by contacting:

WestBow Press
A Division of Thomas Nelson & Zondervan
1663 Liberty Drive
Bloomington, IN 47403
www.westbowpress.com
1 (866) 928-1240

ISBN: 978-1-5127-6560-1 (sc)
ISBN: 978-1-5127-6561-8 (e)

Print information available on the last page.

WestBow Press rev. date: 2/07/2017

Dedicated to my dear mother,
Grace Parker Vinson
1900-1972
Her wonderful story telling laid
a foundation for writing this book.
Special Thanks to
My beloved husband, G. Walton Strickland, Jr.,
for his endless hours of encouragement and typing.
I could not have written this book without him.
To Mother, Anne, Kathy and Willie for their research,
To Willie, Don, Suanne, Keegan and
Mandy for technical assistance,
and to my readers, Charlotte, Golden, Victoria, Paula
Stan, Betty, Scot, Barbara, Jan, and Linda and Carol
Last, but not least,
To Jesus Christ who planted this story in my heart and
made its writing possible.

Prologue

I love watching the drip. . .drip… drip of the raindrops slipping and sliding from one large, glossy magnolia leaf to another. They remind me of my great grandchildren chasing one another on a water slide at one of those fancy water parks they are so fond of. Law me, when we were young we thought it was a real treat just to play in the creek and splash water on each other. Nobody really knows how old the huge magnolia tree is. I'm pretty sure my grand poppa planted it outside the bedroom window on the day my mother was born. Today is my 99th birthday. I can hardly believe it. Huh—I don't feel nearly one hundred years old! Inside this frail, old body, I'm still that adventurous young girl I once was. I had a fine heritage and have had a wonderful life. Now, here I sit here in my favorite, comfortable old chair, just rocking and reminiscing…

My grandmother, Miss Becky, always told me, "Sometimes life changes creep up on us like playful kittens, but other times, they leap on us like roaring lions. With gumption and our Creator's help, we do the best we can." Remembering Grandmother makes me chuckle. She was so tiny, sweet, and gentle, but yet so strong. My momma told me it gave Grand Poppa George pleasure to adore and pamper Miss Becky. In the custom of the Old South he 'protected' her from the business of Silver Lake, their Mississippi plantation. But—when Grand Poppa died in The Great Conflict Between the States, she found herself alone. Only 23 years old, she was now responsible for this large farm, herself, five small children, and a "passel" of slaves.

With much prayer, an iron will, and a strong faith in God, she freed her slaves and then promptly hired them back on sharecropping terms. This way she kept the plantation going. Then she opened 'Miss Becky's Finishing School For Young People' to support and educate her children, as well as those of her friends and neighbors. Momma told me, "I was only a child myself, but I helped my mother in the evenings teach our former slaves to read, write, and to do sums."

I loved hearing mother and Grandmother Becky tell stories from their lives. My own loved ones are delighted when I tell my stories to them. I tell them about what life was like when I was growing up and about their great grand papa, my beloved Tom. I tell them about my great adventure! Would you like to hear my story?

Chapter 1

August 16, 1900

Today is my 18th birthday. I stretch luxuriously, snuggle back into my feather bed and listen to the familiar early morning sounds. Far off, I can hear the tinkling of cowbells as Jabot and Penny, the young Negroes, drive the herd to pasture. Closer, I hear the rumble of wagon wheels and clank of trace-chains as farm machinery rolls through the sandy trails to the cotton fields. Any minute now, I will hear Uncle Bracey whistling "Back to Bethel." Sometimes it's "Beulah Land," but I usually wake up to one melody or the other.

Suddenly, I am fully awake. I sit up in bed and stretch my left hand toward a twinkle of sunlight coming through my window. I turn my hand this way and that, marveling at the magnificent diamond ring Tom placed on my third finger last night. Rainbows of color sparkle on the ceiling and wall. I shiver with delight. This lovely ring once belonged to Tom's grandmother. It fits me perfectly and goes right along with my romantic dreams. For my wedding, I want to wear the lovely silk gown my grandmother and my mother wore for their weddings. I know I love Tom dearly. I can't remember a time when he was not an important part of my life. They say he even held my hand when we were just little tots, and helped me learn to walk.

He has always been my best friend and protector, but when he went away to Law School at "Old Miss," I felt as if part of myself was gone. That was when I realized he had become much more to me than a friend, and I began to dream of a storybook wedding to Tom, my "Prince Charming." I know I'm a responsible, grown woman. Still, I'm just not ready to marry and settle into the role expected of young women in our ultraconservative, sleepy little community in central Mississippi. I want to see how other people live. I want to have some fun and adventure before I settle down into a routine, ordinary life. My heart is set on going to Galveston, "The Playground of the North." I am determined to go there.

In the tall magnolia outside my window, a mockingbird is beginning to sing. I throw back my covers, fling wide the shutters, and give him back trill for trill. It's one of my favorite games. I warble liquid notes and wait. The little bird listens, head cocked first one way and then the other. Not hearing another singer, he resumes his song, then I add a joyful melody. We outdo ourselves in this strange duet. —Uh Oh. I hear heavy footsteps and heavy breathing. Here comes Viney.

"Heah yo' hot water, Nancy honey. Law me, you gonna ketch yo' death o' dampness standin' in that winder half naked. I 'clare to goodness chile, ain't you never gonna learn no shame?" I can't help laughing.

"Viney, my nightgown has long sleeves, reaches to the floor, and buttons up to my chin. All anyone could see is my hands, but you know nobody is going to see me anyway and I do love to tease that bird. He thinks he's such a singer!"

"So he is chile, so he is. But so is you. I 'clare to goodness, de angels must uv dropped yo' voice 'round heah somewhere. It sho ain't human."

"Go on Viney, you're an old angel yourself. You'll have me so vain nobody can stand me."

"Shucks Honey, you ain't vain, but they sho is a site o'foolishness in that haid o' yourn. I declare—."That is as far as she gets. I seize her and swing her around in a wild dance. We both laugh and I gave her a warm hug and kiss her cheek. Viney's like another mother to me. She has been taking care of me my whole life.

"Chile, you know how much I love you, but you gonna be the death uv me yet."

"Aw Mammy, there you go again! You know you wouldn't trade me off for a brass monkey. Now get me out a dress to wear and stop grumbling. Get that new one. You know—."

Viney dutifully opens the ceiling-high wardrobe and lovingly selects a flowered muslin.

"Here you is, honey, now shake yo'self. I got hot cakes and honey waitin', an' time you gets there I'll have a three minute egg an' a big glass o' cold buttermilk to go with it, so hustle," and away she goes to get my breakfast ready.

Sometimes, I wish things would change, but some things I don't ever want to give up.

I look around my room with its honey-colored furniture, (willed to me by Miss Becky) long windows, high ceiling and wide walls. All around me is a lovely unspoiled colonial home. This was one mansion General Sherman missed. It was right on his march of destruction, too. Many times I've heard Poppa,

3

Uncle Bracey, and the other men laugh about the trick that saved it. It is one of my favorite stories.

> "Uncle Bracey was just a young man in his early twenties when he had to leave this home unguarded while he battled in General Lee's army. So they posted a slave on the main road and another at the big gate. The road opened to a slope that led to a dense grove of trees. Beyond the trees, the lane curved around the lake and led to this lovely ancestral home. If Yankee soldiers were spotted, the watchmen would ride like mad, summon other slaves, and swiftly bring headstones from the family burying ground and set them up on the hillside inside the big gate. When General Sherman's raiders followed the lane from the main road, they found a country graveyard set in the dark woods. They just turned around in disgust, never even suspecting the treasure beyond the woods."

So they missed Silver Lake. I just love my home and my heritage. It has cost my family plenty to keep this place…through war and carpetbagging, yellow fever epidemics, riots, graft and confiscatory taxes, Ku-Klux Klan and other lawlessness. Silver Lake is still ours. Our servants are safe and happy, busy at their work, not drifting around like po-white trash wondering where their next meal is coming from. But—sometimes, life is just dull. Oh well, enough daydreaming. If I don't get on down to breakfast, Viney will be coming after me. I nibble Viney's hot cakes, and call to the young family groom, who is in the kitchen, "Joe, when you are through eating, saddle Ginger, please. I'll want him as soon as I've finished breakfast."

"Yas Mam." Joe jumped up and hurried away to the stable. Mother overheard me, and came into the kitchen. "Nancy, if you are riding this morning, I'd like you to take some preserves to Mrs. Lofton and invite them to come for dinner next Sunday after church. It has been several weeks since we've had company. I do hope you're not going to wear that divided skirt again to ride in. My dear, you simply must realize that a southern lady cannot ride around the country astride her horse like a man." *I chuckle to myself and wonder again how Mother can look so severe and commanding and at the same time, be so small, gentle and pretty. She is nearly middle aged, has softly curling chestnut hair and skin as fine and fair as a baby's. She has dignity and a sweet spirit—a sort of goodness neither grief, war, nor reconstruction can destroy. In spite of the limitless quantities of work and detail involved in the management of our vast household, she seems as dainty as a porcelain doll.*

"Well, all right, Mother. I won't wear that skirt. Just to please you, I'll wear this dress."

"That dress looks so nice, dear. It looks fresh and ladylike."

"Oh !" The exclamation escapes her as I, with a straight face, sweep aside the panel on my full skirt and reveal my dress and the ruffled petticoat underneath, divided neatly in two. Mother took a deep breath, exhaled and turned to Viney, her childhood playmate who was born a slave, but is now my beloved Mammy, "Viney, how could you? You know I don't want my daughter to ride astride her horse. How can I ever do anything with her when you spoil her like that."

"Goodness me," Viney tucked her head, "I jes' make it like she tole me to. Oh my—"

And she became very busy clearing the breakfast dishes. I giggle and Mother sighs. She know perfectly well scolding is futile 'cause I can wrap my mammy around my finger and back.

"Never mind, Mama, I know I'm a trial for you, but I'll try not to really disgrace you. Let's have that basket and I'll tell Mrs. Lofton they are invited to come over for a good visit and to help us eat fried chicken this very next Sunday. I see Joe has Ginger ready." I kiss Mother lightly on the cheek, and run down the steps to the mounting block, where Joe is holding my high-spirited horse steady for me to mount.

Chapter 2 – Restless

The sandy road led through old growth scrub oak, and pine forest. The brilliant blue late summer sky made me squint and look ahead for the next patch of shade. Swinging lightly to Ginger's lazy canter, I switch the heads of the bitter weeds with my riding crop. Old Dan, Poppa's long-legged pointer, is exploring afield from one side of the road to the other. Ginger shied away from a blacksnake slipping across the road. Seeing the curving track on the roadbed, reminds me how as a child, I traced such a track with my bare toes, shivers running down my spine, and imagined a rattler or a copperhead might be hidden somewhere nearby. A flash of red through the woods reveals a cardinal and in an old treetop a crow calls 'Caw,caw.' Ginger startles again as quail burst up from a roadside thicket.

"Ah-ha! Scare us would you? Well I wish I had my shotgun, I'd have fried quail for supper." I swiveled in the saddle and whistled to the old bird dog,

"Dan, you lazy rascal, a lot of good you're doing quartering the field way over there, while birds fly up right under our feet." The pointer raced back to me.

When the Lofton's place comes into view, I blow on my

fists. First, a long clear note, then a twirling imitation of a screech owl. Hearing me, Sally returns my whistle and runs down the slope to open the big gate.

"Hello, Nancy! I'm so glad to see you! Do you realize we have been using our secret signal for eleven years? Ever since we were in the second grade and learned how to whistle." We both laugh. "Pull up and let me get up behind you. Ginger has room for one more on his speckled hide. Where did you get that darling dress? My mother would kill me if I rode like that, but the dress is a honey. Did you order it?"

"No, Viney made it for me. Mother nearly had a fit, but she couldn't whip us both, so——," I shrug my shoulders, laugh and dismiss the subject. It always makes me a little sad to ride up to the Lofton place. Beside the garden, the chimney stones and what's left of foundations, show where a lovely home once stood. The remains of cotton houses and carriage house still give mute testimony to what happened here. The family had to take refuge in the corncrib, hidden by overgrown vines, while General Sherman's raiders drove off horses, cattle, and hogs. They scattered the chickens, turkeys, and guineas, raided the potato house and smoke house where the bacon, hams, and sausage hung. They stripped the cellars where jars of vegetables and fruits put up in summer were stored, looted the house of its treasures, and then, burned everything to the ground.

Now, the Lofton's home is just a rambling log structure of native pine with no paint and bare floors, but they don't waste time and energy in self-pity. With faith and southern determination—and the help of friends and neighbors, they built this log house and made the most of what was left to them. Sally doesn't have any inherited treasures. Her house is not beautiful but they are a loving family and make it a good home anyway.

Soon we girls are sitting on the verandah drinking iced tea, and swinging lazily in the slatted swing Mr. Lofton built to hang on this porch. He is very handy with his tools. I delivered the preserves and Mrs. Lofton promises they will visit next Sunday. Sally took a deep breath, wiggled into a comfortable position and smiled.

"Don't you just love these late summer days? I'm sure the air doesn't smell as good anywhere else in the world as it does among the piney woods of Mississippi."

"It's the pine that does it, and the wealth of wild flowers. On the way over here, I saw golden rod and black-eyed-susans blooming everywhere, and don't forget the bitter weeds." I giggled, "They are always with us."

"Well, that's the truth. They say everything in the world is good for something, but the only thing bitter weeds seem to be good for is to make the milk so bitter you can't drink it, if the cows happen to eat them. Maybe some day scientists will find some wonderful use for bitter weeds." We both laugh..

"I love all our seasons. When winter comes the holly berries will be getting red. The chestnuts and chinquapins and hickory nuts will fall, sugar cane and pears will ripen, mistletoe berries will be ivory white." When she said this, Sally wiggled her eyebrows—as if pretending mistletoe really did give the boys permission to kiss us.

"I just love the fall," we said in unison, and burst out laughing at our surprise duet. Remembering an old school girl game, we hooked the little fingers of our right hands, pulled and shouted, "Ditto!" We just swing a while in silence, enjoying the cool breeze on this hot August day.

"I see that far-away look in your eyes, Nancy Norsworthy. I'm used to your musing. I've seen and heard it all before."

"I know, but sometimes life is just so dull. I want to get out on my own—see something of the rest of the world and see how other people live." I glanced over in time to see a beautiful, slender lady walk by carrying a basket of fresh flowers from her garden. Her sunbonnet did not hide the long thick braid of lovely dark auburn hair nor the damp curling wisps that had escaped her braid. I waved and called "Hi, Auntie June."

"Hello Nancy. How are you this fine day? Please tell your sweet mother 'Hello' and give her a hug for me. Excuse me for not stopping to visit. I must get these flowers in some water, before they wilt in this heat." She smiled at me, shading her lovely green eyes with her free hand and hurried into the house.

"Now see, that's what I mean. Take Auntie June for instance. She is the loveliest person and so sweet. But what does she have? There just weren't enough men to go around when the war was over. And here she is, living in other people's lives with no home of her own."

"But we love having her here," Sally protested, "and she wouldn't have married anyone else anyway." Sally looked out at a large oak tree. High on its trunk, and deeply imbedded, a sword hilt protruded from the living wood. "You know when Auntie June's sweetheart, Cliff Summers, went off to war, that tree was just a sapling. He drove his sword into it and told her he would be as true to her as that sword was fast in the wood. It was to remain there as his pledge until he came back and removed it. Well, he died at the battle of Antietam—and no one could remove the sword now. Auntie June would never forget Cliff. He was her true love."

"But you don't have to worry about finding a husband. All the boys in the county are crazy about you. And Tom Huggins—Well!" Sally pretended to blush, flicked her eyebrows up and down and fanned her face with her hand. "That ring is gorgeous, and so is Tom." She giggled.

"I know. Tom is my best friend and I've always loved him—but I want to live. I want to experience dancing to a real orchestra, and laughter, rich surroundings, and people who are charming and free. You know where I want to go—to Galveston, The Playground of the North."

"Galveston? My goodness! Father says that's a mighty wicked place—with drinking and gambling and all sorts of wild living!"

"I don't care. I intend to go there. I think Momma and Poppa are stuffy about drinking. Why, really cultured people all drink, don't they? And, if people want to play with their own money, what of it? I'm tired of being so straight-laced. This is a new century. Things are changing. I want to have some fun."

"Well, I think we do have fun. We ride and hunt, and visit with each other. And our dances—you know they're fun. And our picnics and hay rides—"

"Our dances? Just our own little crowd, with a local band for music. No public dances, chaperones hovering, and not even a drop of wine in the punch. I want some adventure and real fun. I'm going to Galveston. You just wait and see."

Chapter 3 – Congregating

Saturday bustled with activity because our family, and the Silver Lake servants as well, went to church on Sunday. The day before the Sabbath everyone did double duty. House cleaning, begun on Friday, finished on Saturday. Every garment must be in order, from those of the family to those of smallest child. The kitchen staff hustled, getting chickens dressed and ready to fry, cakes, cookies, pies, and bread baked. I oversaw such tasks as Mother asked of me, made my own preparations for the Sabbath, and reluctantly did my regular job, the family mending.

While I stitch, I ponder. *Mother taught me it was lady-like to give the impression of fragile tenderness. She also held that I must learn to be a keen and efficient housewife. She never seems to realize the difficulty of reconciling that huge accomplishment with a deceptively meek personality. Mother does it–she is both genteel and efficient. I was reared in southern tradition, but I have difficulty accepting this paradox graciously. I am expected to be well read, play at least one instrument, and sing. I can paint acceptably, ride, garden, and "sew a fine seam." I must, also, give meticulous care to my own health and beauty, take thought for the wellbeing of others, be a cheerful and pleasant companion, and at the same time keep skillful control of an immense amount of detail. All this while sharing and directing prodigious amounts of work. Fatigue is a word I never hear mentioned. Mother's concession to human limits is an hour spent lying down in the darkness of her room every afternoon, with a cool cloth over her eyes.*

Guided by Mother, I am learning to balance all this work with the art of living. In my plantation home, my parents shield me and I feel loved by every servant on the place. I know, now that I am more mature, I am naïve, sheltered from the darker side of society, but I know it is there. I'm eighteen. I believe I can handle whatever I encounter, and I cherish my own ideal dreams. Why can't I just be Me?

Sunday dawned clear, with a cloudless sky. Scripture reading and prayer followed breakfast, then every one scattered to dress for Sunday services. About nine o'clock, household noises die out as the servants finish their tasks and hurry to their cabins to get their own families off to meetin'. Soon I can see them from my window, dressed in their best clothes, singing, gesturing happily, and greeting new groups that join them as they all walk along the lane. Around the bend, the bell begins to ring in the steeple of their beloved little white church. It was built of wide heart-pine boards in the days when their forebears had been slaves. Hearing the bell's call, they pick up their pace, hustling the children along to Sunday School.

"Are you ready, Nancy?" Mother calls. Catching up my lace mitts, fan, lace edged handkerchief and bag, I hurry down to where Lige holds the reins for the prancing, snorting team, hitched to the two seated, fringed-top surrey. When I am settled in behind my parents, Poppa clucks to the horses, flips the reins and we are off on our two-mile journey to Clear Creek Church. The road is a narrow track, winding around deep gullies, uphill and down. Sometimes we pass over hard red clay and sometimes through whispering ruts of sand.

Even as a child I loved the time when the horses, Sam and Charley, after a quick look, step down into the shallow creek, and stop to swill a cool drink of water before stepping out on the other side. Poppa explains, "In that swift moment, horses seem to know by instinct whether a bridge or a stream is safe. Sometimes by their refusal to proceed, the horses save their owners from disaster."

I love to hear these tales of experiences my father and his friends exchange while they sit by the fireplace on long winter evenings or on the breezy verandah in the summer. Now the wheels are whispering down through the shallow water so clear you can see the colored stones in the creek bed. Soon we draw up before the beloved church named for that Clear Creek.

The long cool room with its vaulted ceiling has been part of my life as far back as I can remember. Inside, there is a hush among our people—a peacefulness that seeps into my being. There is no cold ceremony, or carping puritanism here, but an atmosphere of understanding and affection. Our unity inspires faith and security. We young people are quiet out of reverence, and even the small children feel it. They sit so quietly they often fell asleep. Occasionally, one of the older men falls asleep also and I get tickled if someone snores, but I dare not giggle out loud. I particularly love the sound of the foot-pedaled organ, and the rhythm of the men in prayer. Women do not pray aloud in church. The mellow voices of our friends and neighbors thrill my soul as they sing,

"How firm a foundation, Ye saints of the Lord!
Is laid for your faith, In His excellent Word."

The Methodists hold services in the Clear Creek Church on the first and third Sundays of the month, and the Baptists hold sway on the second and fourth Sundays. When there is a fifth Sunday in the month, a joint singing and "dinner on the grounds" is celebrated. It is hard to say which I enjoy the most, the extra music, or the fellowship. I cherish them both. Out under the trees, wide planks are laid across sawhorses to make long tables. These are then covered with crisp white sheets for tablecloths. Every cook in the county brings her very best casseroles and desserts. We always have fried chicken, smoked hams, fresh tomatoes, "roastin' ears of corn," green beans, juicy watermelon, cornbread, cakes and pies of every description—a veritable feast. Yum! Cool water from the nearby spring provides refreshing drinks for all.

After everyone has eaten their fill, the children play, little ones and the older men nap, and young sweethearts stroll hand in hand while the women pack away the multitude of "left overs." Nothing is wasted. Then, we all gather for the singing, accompanied by organ, piano, violins, banjos, and guitars. Sally and I sing our favorite duet, 'In The Garden,' accompanied by Tom on his violin. Poppa, Mr. Lofton, Tom and his brother Mack close the program with a quartet, 'The Old Rugged Cross,' in perfect harmony. It is late afternoon when everyone gets ready to make their way home. We are weary of body, but lighter of soul. Still, cows have to be milked, chickens fed, all the usual chores done and preparation made for school on Monday.

This faith and strength conquered a wilderness, drove back savages, pestilence, fought turmoil, and war and came out on the other side triumphant. These kinds of neighbors become friends as close as brothers. Here is the unity that makes this nation great. "Under God." That was it, even if Abraham Lincoln did say it! I look around the great room. Through the open windows the sun streams in. Hand held fans, made of palmetto, pasteboard, or fabric, sing soft swishing sounds, coaxing the breeze to cool the summer air. I look at the faces, stern and manly, clear-eyed and keen, soft and feminine like my mother's, or work-worn and gaunt like some of the older folks. These individuals, though they are all different are alike somehow. Kindness and respect is in them all. They may not all agree on every issue, but each one matters to the others. Even with their unrelenting moral standards, these people are loving and any one of them would share their last crust of bread. This Christianity is real.

It amuses me that Baptist or Methodist, the little church is filled with the same worshippers week after week. Even with my heart full of the deep, beloved peace about me, I am conflicted—my mind slips back to my old, cherished dream—*getting out on my own, seeing how other people live, have some real fun and a little adventure in my life.* Somewhere I intend to find it. I hear in Galveston–New Orleans is too Frenchie. It wouldn't be the same. Mobile is too close to home. My heart is set on Galveston. I will talk to Mother tonight.

The stir of arising for the last prayer brings me back from my reverie and I bow my head with the rest for Brother Armes' deep-voiced benediction. "Grace, mercy, and peace from God our Father be with you all. Amen!."

Chapter 4 – Company

The Loftons are coming for Sunday lunch. They are quite a large family. Besides Mr. and Mrs. Lofton, Auntie June, Wayne, and Sally, there are five younger children who sit on a blanket in the bottom of the Lofton's wagon. The older Loftons occupy the two spring seats. "Jelly (Angelica) Price, Wayne's girlfriend, and Tom and Mack Huggins are coming, also. After the worship service, we make a merry parade as we all get underway. The three girls ride in the back seat of the surrey, the three young men on horseback, ride to each side, and the Lofton's wagon follows. Topping the long hill of red clay, we leave the big road and follow the sandy trail through the pine trees to our main gate. Just as Jabot opens it for us to pass through, the bay horse happens to open his long mouth in a yawn that bares all his teeth. The little boy looked up into that yawning chasm and shrieked, "Help, dat debils gonna get me!" and he ran as fast as he could. Tom laughed so hard, he almost fell off his horse, but dropped behind and closed the gate. "Goosing" his horse into a canter, he arrived in time to assist us girls as we jumped down from the surrey's high step.

"Welcome! Come in!" urged Colonel Norsworthy. As the

company moved toward the house, he held the door open. "Come right on in. Viney, take the gentlemen's hats. Ladies, follow Mrs. Norsworthy. She will show you what to do with your purses and things. Everyone, please be seated be seated. I will open the blinds so the sunshine can come in. Is everybody comfortable? We will have cold fruit juice punch in a minute. Viney makes it of juices put up in the summer—dewberry, peach, and scuppernong, served with lemon and mint. We find it quite refreshing. Here she comes now. Thank you, Viney. That looks good."

"Looks good?" said Sally, "Just wait 'til you taste it, Umm!" Viney entered with a heavy silver tray laden with slender glasses. The glasses had been chilled in the deep well before being filled with the cool juice. When all had been served, and had sipped the delicious nectar, Viney was sincerely complimented on her refreshment.

"I wonder if we could have some music before dinner, Nancy. I haven't heard that lovely voice in quite awhile." Mr. Lofton turned to Nancy's father. "You know Sam, her voice is really quite extraordinary. I have never heard anything like it outside the concert stage. I wonder sometimes ..."

"Oh no." Mr. Norsworthy quickly answered, "Nancy would never care to sing in public. God gave her voice to give pleasure, not to commercialize it. Such a life would be entirely unsuited to her. It is enough for her to give happiness with her singing. Isn't that right, daughter? Will you sing for us now?"

"Of course. But Sally must play for me. And what shall I sing? Your favorite, 'Bells of Shamoney' or Mr. Lofton's favorite, 'Highland Lassie'?"

Sally broke in, "No, lets do mine first—'The Bell Song.'" Soon the summer air was alive with melody.

Poppa pointed to the window. On an oak limb my mockingbird friend was trilling along with me. I went to the window and the lilting give and take with the bird continued, back and forth from girl to bird, sometimes together. It was a familiar game to my family and friends.

"And now for Mr. Lofton's favorite—I began to sing an old melody, "Oh where, oh where has my lassie gone?" Tom picked up the violin and joined the music.

The noon meal was served., we feasted on fried chicken, hot biscuit with fresh butter, rice and cream gravy, vegetable salads, tomatoes fresh from the vines, and sweets of every description— more food than could be consumed by even a crowd such as this one. Gracious manners, laughter, and good conversation added to the pleasure of the occasion. Long after the meal was finished we lingered talking. Mr. Lofton, a slender grey-haired man with intense blue eyes, had not forgotten the battles of the tragic war nor the heartache that followed. He and Poppa retired to the library with their pipes and recounted the days of reconstruction and the tribulation and chaos in its aftermath. Some of the young people played chess, backgammon or Rook. Others went out and played croquet or sat in the swings and visited.

Twilight came. At last I was alone in my room. Mother would be along soon to say goodnight. It had been a long, happy day. Lingering after the others, Tom had again begged me to set a date for our marriage, but I did not. I know I am blessed with love and a comfortable life but I cannot settle into it because of my restless dream. I heard mother's light steps and then a soft knock, "You still up darling? It has been a nice day hasn't it? There is nothing better than a day with one's friends. I could see by Tom's face that you put him off again. What is it, daughter? If you are not sure you love him—"

"I do love him, Mother, but I am not ready to settle down. I just want a chance to see what life is like in other places. Oh Mother, I want to experience some adventure. I want to waltz to a real orchestra, see a real opera! Didn't you go to fancy balls and such before you were married? When you were away from home in college, didn't you have some adventure? What about before Poppa went to war? What about, "the Romance of the Ante Bellum South" I've heard about all my life?" A peculiar expression crossed Mother's face.

"Yes, dear, I remember the night Sam went away. There was a big ball. The girls wore lovely gowns and the men were in uniform. It was all very exciting. Do you remember those gilded epaulets of your father's? He looked so dashing and handsome with them on the shoulders of his uniform. We were young and full of romance. We had no idea of the realities of war. But you must try to understand, dear. We have lived through bitter times. Your father and I have learned there is a more lasting happiness than gaiety, which just lives on the surface. One does not survive war and reconstruction, epidemics, struggles, and disaster, without recognizing that some aids to merriment simply weigh down the human race. 'A merry heart makes a glad countenance' is true, but some aids to laughter turn to dull eyes and headaches in the morning. Those antique gowns, jewelry, and their stories handed down to you are souvenirs. Everything they represent belongs to an age that is *gone*, but the true good life goes on. What better romance could you want than that which lasts as long as life lasts, and what better fun, than a life full of love, goodness, and laughter?" Reaching out, I hugged my mother.

"I know, 'Miss Fancy', I know you're right—but I just need to see, and make choices for myself. Please let me go! I shall never be happy unless I see Galveston. I'm simply beating my wings. I shall never be satisfied until I go. I come from a long line of strong women. I can take care of myself. I'll be all right!"

Her mother looked at her shrewdly. "Perhaps you are right, dear. We have friends in New Orleans, and in Mobile—"

"Mobile! That's right in our back yard! I want to get completely away, Mother. My heart is set on Galveston!"

"Galveston! Why, Nancy! That is said to be the wickedest place in the southland. It is where all the rich Northerners go to winter, drink, and gamble. Your father would never—"

"Oh Mother! I think father is stuffy about such things. He is so serious—and narrow! So many things are fun if they're not made harmful. And they don't have to be. Why Grandpoppa George and Grandmother Becky had toddies and juleps and wines—when they were young didn't they? They didn't think everything was *sinful*. Father has just become straight-laced. He is *just dull!*"

"*Nancy!* Your father, dull? With his merry-hearted wit and humor, his kindness, and charm?" Incredulous, she shook her head.

"Oh I know, mother. I didn't mean to step on your toes, but he is *stuffy* about liquor and such. And Galveston! Well I don't believe it's so wicked. People just go there to have a good time—to be happy. Momma... I just have to go —to see for myself."

Mrs. Norsworthy went back to Nancy's first remark.

"Not stuffy, Nancy, just clear-headed. Your father has lived in troublesome times. He and his friends have had to fight for our good way of life, and in the process have discarded those things which do nobody any good and can cause so much harm. They have learned that you cannot compromise on some things. If given any place, they color all. They have seen how liquor and the gambling craze can be used to enslave whole segments of the population, how the basest human emotions are released under their influence. They have removed these elements from our environment, and the result is not loss, but gain." Mother busied herself turning down the bed and carefully folding the hand tucked pillow sham.

"I wish you would be more thoughtful of your father, Nancy. He loves you dearly, and feels you are the jewel of our proud family heritage. I'm afraid you hurt him deeply when you speak as if you are not happy in your home. The two little graves on the hillside, your brothers who were lost in the yellow fever epidemic, no doubt intensify his feelings, but such an attitude as you are expressing would hurt him, as you know."

I burst into tears. Mother understood my high-strung temperament very well. She patted my head. I leaned against her and looked up.

"Mother, please, I simply have to go."

"Perhaps you do, daughter. You must see for yourself, and decide for yourself. I only hope it will not be too much of a change for you."

"Then you'll talk to Poppa?"

"Leave your father to me. Aunt Grace Hand lives in Galveston. I will write her tomorrow."

"I will write to Mrs. Hand—' Mother, can't you understand, I want to get out on my own."

"Nancy, you will either visit the Hands or you positively shall not go! It is enough to let you go under any circumstances."

"Oh, all right. I'll visit the Hands! But I want to go *now*. Right away."

Mother laughed. "Not so fast. We need to shop in Jackson, and we will have to wait until we hear from them before you go." "Yes, mother! But let's make it soon." I began to wiggle with anticipation. Impulsively I hugged mother again.

"Then I can really go?"

"Yes, dear, as soon as I can arrange it." Sighing—"I'll go break the news to your father."

"Wheeee!" Whirling in a wild dance I landed in the middle of my feather bed. Mother quietly closed the door as she left.

Later, in the downstairs library, Mrs. Norsworthy approached her husband with a cup of warm sassafras tea and the news. She encountered just the reaction she had anticipated.

"Anne! What on earth are you thinking? Galveston! Of all places. I won't have it. She simply cannot go."

"Yes, dear, I think she must. I know it's a wicked city, and as Uncle Walt says, 'one day God will wipe it off the map like Sodom and Gomorrah,' but Nancy's heart is set and I think we had better let her go."

"But she is such a child, mother, far younger than her years. So sweet and unspoiled to be off there meeting all sorts of people. Why, it makes me weak to think of all that could happen to her. Everything will be so foreign to her way of life."

"That's just it. We have shaped her carefully, and now she must try her wings. She is a child of intense emotions, full of the romance of the Old South. She would always feel that she had missed something. She would always remain unsatisfied if we did not allow her to make this experiment. She would always think our good way of life terribly dull. We can only hope that our training will stand her in good stead and she will see clearly when she judges for herself. Perhaps, she will come back to us ready to settle down with Tom and be happy in the ways that leave no regrets. Anyway—I feel it is a risk we must take, lonely as we will be when she is gone." Poppa thought it over and looked up at Mother with a wry smile.

"All right, Miss Fancy. That head is awful dainty to hold such a deal of wisdom. You always get your way in the end, and you are seldom wrong. Go on and write Grace Hand. Shop and spend some money on our daughter. But, Viney goes to watch over her and that is final."

"Very well, dear. That is a good idea. Viney goes with her my darling."

Dropping a kiss on the top of his head, she smiled. When her husband or her daughter called her "Miss Fancy", she knew she had won her point.

Chapter 5 – Jackson

At my insistence, we quickly made preparation for a shopping excursion to Jackson. Since we could count on clear weather this time of the year, we would make the trip in the surrey instead of on the train. Poppa would accompany us and attend to business in the capital while we shopped. Since Viney was needed at home, young Mandy would go along to help the ladies. Our travel would take two days each way. By leaving early, we could stop over and visit Cousin Frank Warren's family at Stonehaven. We cherished these rare opportunities to "catch up" with those dear to us. Perhaps, I could persuade my cousin, Florence, to go with us to the capital. It would be fun to have another girl my age along on the trip.

* * * * *

As we approached Jackson, I felt a delicious shiver of excitement. The history of my state fascinated me. The fine old Statehouse with its great dome and arched doorways sat among magnificent old oak trees. Long and thrilling history took place here, from the time of the Indians even until today. Oh, the stories this site could tell, if only the trees could talk.

The treaty of Dancing Rabbit Creek had been signed here, bringing peace between white settlers and Choctaw Indians. One of my ancestors had signed the treaty, along with the great Indian Chiefs Pushmataha and Puckshenubbe. My grandmother, Miss Becky told me the story.

When she was just a very little girl, her grandfather had been instrumental in bringing about the treaty. I loved to hear her tell her stories and to imagine myself participating in these historical events. These kinds of personal histories are seldom included in history books. This story is another one of my favorites.

"A great feast was prepared out under the ancient oak trees. No stone was left unturned, for the future of the settlers depended on the goodwill of the two great and powerful Indians, Chief Pushmataha and Chief Puckshenubbe. Long tables were set up and covered with white sheets used as table cloths. A great variety of carefully prepared food was spread on the tables. Suspended from a tree limb above the tables hung a beautiful fan made of peacock feathers. A small slave girl pulled a silken rope to swing the fan back and forth, swishing the air and keeping flies away from the food. The two great chiefs were seated in the places of honor. All was going well until little Sulu, the slave child, laid down her silken rope, picked up a napkin and wiped the grease dripping from Chief Pushmataha's chin. A unified intake of breath and alarmed silence gave evidence of their fear that the powerful man had been offended. Rather than offending him, the great chief was flattered at the child's attention and following the dinner, the important treaty was signed by all—including my Great Grandfather."

In this capital, many brave, early struggles took place. Religious freedom, free schools, humane treatment and legal rights for slaves, imprisonment for debts was outlawed, and other important legislative battles were won here. For me, history came alive, as I pictured great statesmen like Jefferson Davis, Henry Clay, and many others legislating in this assembly. The Governor's Mansion had even become headquarters for the hated Yankee, General Sherman, on his destructive "March to the Sea." Because General Sherman occupied it, the manse escaped the wanton destruction that befell so many other beautiful structures. I could hardly wait to walk these historic halls.

Before nightfall, we travelers arrived, and were welcomed to the home of Papa's sister, Lucille Edwards. Papa had planned to engage a groom to bring the surrey from the livery stable and drive us ladies on our shopping excursions the next morning, but young Mr. Edwards requested that privilege. Papa laughed and of course gave his permission.

When we sat at dinner that night, after a day full of shopping, Poppa wanted to know, "Have you bought suitable attire for a formal evening? We are all invited to attend a ball given in the Governor's honor at Rosemont on Saturday night, and I want you to do us credit. The Governor's son has asked if he may be your escort for the evening."

"Wow Poppa! A Ball, at Rosemont, the Governor's mansion? Rosemont has the reputation of being the most beautiful residence in our state, and with the governor's son to escort me?"

"Then I take it you will be pleased with Mr. Longino as an escort?"

I pretended great dignity, "You may assume, Miss Norsworthy accepts." My dignity fled as I told my father excitedly, "Just as soon as dinner is finished, I want to show you the lovely things we bought. Mother, do you think we should show our bounty to him?"

"I'm sure he will be delighted," Mother replied, eyes twinkling, "as long as he does not look too closely at my bank book."

"Oh, don't worry, Miss Fancy, I shall not restrict you there. After all, we have only *one* daughter." I winked at mother and leaned over to hug Poppa. "And she's just about the finest little daughter you have, named *Nancy*, isn't she?"

Chapter 6 – Vicksburg

The next morning, Uncle Robert, Aunt Lucille, and Jack took us on a tour of Vicksburg. We viewed the famous battleground, the caves in which people hid to escape the invading Yankees, and the everlasting scars of battle. We saw the old Warren County Courthouse with its majestic ionic columns and its cannon scars. They showed us the home of Dr. Bodley, one of Vicksburg's crusading editors who was murdered by river-front gamblers for defending the "moral fiber" of the city. Aunt Lucille told us Thomas Jefferson had delivered several important speeches from Dr. Bodley's balcony. We girls "oohed and ahhed" at the elegant red brick homes set nearly three stories high above the street. One home, approached by a flight of white steps with elaborate wrought iron banisters, displayed the same intricate pattern of ironwork on the banisters of its first and second level verandas and again around the edge of the roof.

"Oh! How beautiful! Can't you just imagine the view from that upper gallery. It must be breathtaking," I exclaimed.

"I can imagine," Florence agreed. "With the city all spread below it and the river stretched out in the distance beyond the trees…"

"Would you like to see that view?" Uncle Robert asked.

"Oh, yes. Do you suppose we could?"

"Sure. They are good friends of our family. In fact, we are all invited to one of the magnificent balls they are holding next week. Come along, I'm sure Miss Netty will not mind showing her home. She is very proud of it." Everyone climbed the grand sweep of steps and we were welcomed into the beautiful mansion. We quickly saw that the outside grandeur was matched by the home's interior. Our hostess led us through the points of interest, and before long we were on the magnificent sweeping gallery, looking out over a view which nearly took my breath away. *Here it is, my dream of ante bellum glory, alive. Those beauties and gallants of yore stood right here.* I stood with my hands on the railing, the world sweeping away like fairyland far below. My imagination swirled like the fragrant breeze that swept around us, and carried me far away. It was like coming back from a trance to wrench myself back to the present.

"A penny for your thoughts, Nancy," said Uncle Robert. "I had to speak the third time before you heard me."

"Oh, I'm sorry. I imagined being a guest at a ball given here about fifty years ago. I saw lovely ladies and their escorts, even heard the violins. I imagined they were having a wonderful time."

"Well, you had better come back to the present. We want to show you the Klein home before it gets too late. There is still much to see."

"Do you mean there are other houses like this?" I exclaimed.

"Just you wait and see."

"I am spellbound now. I can't imagine another home as amazing as this."

"Oh," put in Aunt Lucille, "brace yourself. There is more in store, I can tell you that."

We thanked our gracious hostess, bid her good-bye and were on our way.

In a few minutes, Jack drew up before another lovely home. This one was very different, yet every bit as beautiful as the first. Set high upon a terraced hillside, surrounded by huge trees and lovely shrubbery, this mansion had three sections set off by four massive Corinthian columns. Amazing ironwork was repeated in this fence and in the balconies surrounding the center wing of the vast house, just as the previous home had. Medallions as lacy as spider webs ornamented this ironwork. To the left of the main house stood a summerhouse or pavilion, surrounded by a fence of the same exquisite design. Behind the soaring columns, the veranda lay deep and cool. Along its length were Venetian shutters opening the entire length of the wall right onto the luxurious porch. While we waited at the door, I turned toward the street and caught my breath, again. The lawn, with its great statues, swept to a breath-taking view of the mighty Mississippi River.

"Why, we are right over the river, aren't we?"

"Oh, yes! Before the war, these grounds stretched right down to the riverbank, but that has gradually given way to streets, lined with other homes. Outside, this estate has changed, but the inside of the house has not altered much since the days when the mighty Mississippi River came right by here. Jefferson Davis spent many happy hours as a guest in this home and many other famous names engraved on our nation's history were also spoken here." By this time a portly old butler had ushered us courteously inside.

Both Florence and I gasped at the grandeur. Magnificent

furniture and perfect appointments of every kind, in exquisite and perfect taste stood before us. In every direction, mirrors with heavy golden cornices and frames, massive and impressive, extended from ceiling to floor. So perfectly did they fit their wall spaces, it was evident they had been crafted to order. Tapestries, furniture, and rugs, gathered from all over the world, combined in elegant harmony. I, a devotee of the old south found myself again, lost in a spell. The culture of these people, like myself and yet so different, fascinated me.

"No wonder the South fought so valiantly. Imagine homes like this being shelled by attacking cannon."

Our hostess pointed out, "Right here, is one of the shells fired from the river." With horror, I saw the cannonball still embedded in the handcarved woodwork, a web of cracks radiating from it. I did not want to imagine the terror of the residents under attack. Moving on to other portions of the house, she showed the lovely back entrance, where the drive swept up on a gentle curve beneath the portico. Here, ladies might step down from their carriages without exposure to the elements.

The slave cabins lay further back. Finally, our gracious hostess led us out to what seemed to be a small hill on the beautifully landscaped back lawn. The air was fragrant with the scent of roses, azaleas and other flowering shrubs. There were wrought iron benches where one could sit and look over the landscape. A flight of stone steps curved up to this summit. We enchanted girls exclaimed over the view. Then our hostess lifted the limbs of a large rose-colored azalea that lay close to the ground and showed us a large iron disc. When lifted, it gave access to a comfortable underground room!

"In this secret room, the family hid, secure during Yankee

raids," our sweet hostess explained. "I was only a child, and the noise of the cannons was very frightening."

It would be an understatement to say we were in awe of all we had observed, but our tour was not over yet. Back in the carriage, we continued.

"Over there, along the river bank, the flatboat men from the river hung out in "Catfish Row." Those men, referred to as 'ring-tailed tooters,' boasted they could 'throw down, drag out, and lick any man in the country." Professional gamblers, bootleggers, liquor dealers, and soft quadroons, (ladies of the night) added to the melee. Sometimes hired wagon drivers and other ruffians wearing coarse, homemade garments and broad brimmed hats, carrying long plaited rawhide whips, roamed this area. They might be the type to visit the brawling river front, or the brawny patriot type, but one thing they all had in common was scorn for the educated broadcloth suit, high-hat type of city dweller. Sometimes these rowdy groups liquored up and roared through town, popping their long whips like pistol shots and sounding their yodeling sort of 'holler.'"

"I've heard that yodel," I exclaimed. "All the boys at home try to master it at one time or another, and some of them become really good at it. It is a singing sort of yell that changes key in the middle. We can tell which boy it is by the quality of his voice and the distinctive pattern of his yodel."

"Is that what they call the Rebel yell?" Florence asked. "Not hardly!" laughed Aunt Lucille. "The Rebel Yell is something else again. You'd never forget that one if you heard it. Many a Yankee hearing it, dove for cover during the war."

We all laughed. Jack drove along a drive high above the river bluffs. As I looked down the riverbank, my imagination could almost conjure those rowdy days of yore. Imagining I could hear the crack of whips and hear that distinctive yell brought a shiver down my spine.

Jack continued, "This city was a cotton port. It had gins and compresses, warehouses, factories, barge lines and river steamers. They picked up cotton, hardwood lumber, and cattle and brought in treasures from all over the world." Driving on, we saw a great river of sand in a vast channel where the river had once run.

"But—I thought I read that General Grant failed in his efforts to divert the river?"

"He did, but whether the result of his efforts, or just one of those quirks of nature, in 1876 the river changed its channel all by itself. It left our city and all its canals and warehouses high and dry."

"My goodness! That must have been a blow to the whole city."

"It was indeed. And coming so soon after the destruction of war, it certainly called for everything the people of our city had in the way of staying-power." Quietly, Florence and I contemplated such disaster.

"But you know," Aunt Lucille told us, "Jack, has 'a bee in his bonnet' about that. He believes a chain of lakes where he and his cronies sometimes go fishing can be joined together by the use of a canal. The Yazoo River could be turned into that channel and the city could become a live Port again."

"That would be incredible! Why doesn't somebody do it?"

"Well, nobody took him seriously when he piped up with that at the dinner table several years ago. But he still believes it can be done. Jack is almost through engineering school. It wouldn't surprise me to see him try it one of these days."

Jack's face was red, "I will try it one of these days. Not only try, but I will do it!" Wanting to encourage him, I blurted,

"Wouldn't that be wonderful? You keep right on believing it can be done and we'll be pulling for you. One of these days, we'll keep a date we make today, for a river steamer trip. We will be picked up *right here!*"

"It's a date." Jack agreed. "Now folks, we'd better head home. Your parents must be wondering what in the world has become of us. You girls don't want to be worn out before the ball tomorrow night and you surely don't want to miss your beauty naps." He ducked as the girls pretended they would whack him. Laughing, he turned the horses toward home. "You'll want to get your best 'bib and tuckers' ready and have your dancing shoes all tuned up before tomorrow."

"Thank you so much for the tour of those beautiful homes. Neither of us will ever forget this day!" Jack nodded and grinned as he drove away to stable the horses.

Chapter 7 – The Ball

A bright full moon silvered all I could see. Aunt Lucille said, "The moon is shining no brighter than the excitement in your eyes, my dear." It seemed to me I had been dressed and ready to go for hours. Aunt Lucille had swept my golden blond hair up into a coronet of curls and woven tiny fragrant sweetheart roses into the braid. My new gown of iridescent moire taffeta in rich brown with copper highlights was the perfect complement to the antique topaz jewelry passed down to me by Miss Becky. An off-the-shoulder sweetheart neckline showed my creamy skin, revealing only a few freckles. Poppa thinks my freckles charming, but I wish they would fade away. The flair of my skirt, made bouffant by rows and rows of tulle ruffles on my petticoat accented my tightly laced tiny waist. I felt like a princess.

Florence, who was to be escorted by Jack, wore a pale blue satin gown which matched her large sapphire eyes. Its gored skirt swept to a short train, fastened at the back of her waist with a large flat bow. An exquisite Italian cameo on a black velvet ribbon graced Florence's slender neck.

"Look, Mother," I cried, as I caught cousin Florence's hands and twirled us both about,

"I feel like Cinderella about to go to the Ball!" Poppa spoke around a lump in his throat,

"I am glad you are not wearing any other jewelry than your heirlooms tonight, my darling daughter. They would only detract from your natural radiance."

"Oh Poppa"—I felt an embarrassing blush, and hugged him gingerly to avoid crushing my dress or the fine hairdressing Aunt Lucille had prepared for me.

At last, my proud parents and our hosts, announced, "It is time for us to go."

* * * * *

The carriage entered the lane leading to Rosemont's circular drive, where our horses joined a long queue of other carriages. I didn't mind the wait, for there was much to see. Magnificent magnolia trees with large, gleaming white blossoms and glossy leaves reflected the moonlight. As we neared the Governor's mansion, Rosemont, I exclaimed,

"Look! It must be lit with a million candles." In the center of the circular drive, an elegant fountain sent up jets of water, sparkling like diamonds in the flickering light from tall lanterns. Sweet, exotic fragrance from tiers of lovely roses mingled with the scent of pines. As our carriage arrived at the entrance, two stately doormen, clad in scarlet uniforms trimmed with gold braid and ornate gold buttons approached. Bowing low and opening the doors, they extended white-gloved hands to assist the ladies as we daintily stepped from the carriage onto crimson carpet runners. I looked up into a pair of shining dark eyes. A tall handsome young man with a mass of curly dark hair extended his own white-gloved hand to lead me up the curved sweep of marble steps.

"You are Miss Nancy Norsworthy, I believe. I am Hugh Longino. With your permission, it is my privilege and delight to be your escort this evening."

"Thank you sir. I am indeed Nancy, and you are most gracious to welcome a stranger to your home." Entering through a magnificent carved archway, my breath caught in my throat at the wonders before me. Our party paused before entering the ballroom. An orchestra seated on an elevated dais to our left played a Beethoven selection. The lovely room, filled with ladies in exquisite gowns and men in elegant evening wear made me feel I was finally experiencing my dreams of gay antebellum days. Suddenly, I heard the page announce,

"Colonel and Mrs. Robert Jackson English." He was about to introduce my parents and myself. Hugh at my elbow, gently moved me forward.

"Colonel and Mrs. Samuel Elijah Norsworthy."

"Miss Nancy Anne Norsworthy and Mr. Hugh Parker Longino."

Still feeling like Cinderella, I gracefully (I hope) descended the curved stairs and Hugh led me to a beautifully appointed table at the edge of the dance floor. He bowed slightly.

"May I have this dance, Miss Nancy?" I smiled and extended my gloved hand. We waltzed in graceful rhythm. Hugh led me in the slow turns and smooth glides with perfection. As we started back to our table near the chaperones, a tall, handsome man, bowing with exaggerated courtliness, confronted me.

"May I have the pleasure of this dance?" Astonished at this unexpected presence, I was momentarily speechless.

"Cousin Tom!" Hugh exclaimed, "Welcome! I had no idea

you were in Jackson. Apparently, you have met my lovely new friend, Miss Nancy Norsworthy."

"Yes," Tom answered. "I believe we have met before. I just decided this would be a good time for me to visit Jackson, and upon arriving, I found no one at home at the Edwards'. So, learning you were all at Rosemont, I decided to call on you, my dear distant cousin Hugh, and … Here I am!"

"I see, you rascal," Longino laughed. "Sly fellow, aren't you? Well—it is always a pleasure to see you."

"The pleasure is all mine, Hugh. I see we seem to have similar interests." Tom smiled as he nodded toward me.

"Yes, of course." Hugh motioned to a young fellow coming toward them from across the room. "Lamar, I see this is supposed to be your next dance, but since you have another dance down the way, may I suggest you relinquish this one to Mr. Huggins? It seems he has ridden half way across the state for a dance. It would be a shame for him to miss it."

"Oh shoot! Here I finagle a dance from the prettiest girl in the country, and I have to give it up to some dance-hungry Paul Revere." The young men all laughed and introductions followed. With my permission, Lamar, with goodnatured grumbling, relinquished his place on my dance card to Tom. I was delighted to dance this two-step with my sweetheart.

Exhilarated by the heady atmosphere of Rosemont, the music, and the surprise of Tom's presence, I breathed deeply and said, "Whew, Tom, this music goes to my head—or maybe to my feet. Wouldn't you just love to let go and dance a jig like a couple of wild country kids?"

"Hmmm, we'll do that sometime," he replied—"but probably not in the ballroom at Rosemont. What would the governor's son think if his demure little friend should suddenly break into a country jig?" I laughed, but with effort, maintained my decorum.

"Of course. It was just an idea. But honestly, I'm all churned up inside. I want to dance like the wind and sing to the top of my voice in the moonlight."

"Uh Oh, Here comes another one of those Mississippi riverbank rebels to claim his dance with you. You'd better anchor those feet more firmly and dim those eyes a little or you might just go to his head. You are intoxicating enough as it is," Tom teased. I blushed and smiled.

"Oh, I know how to behave. Just watch me. It's only with you, Tom, that I can freely express how I really feel."

Just before my partner whisked me away, Tom reached for my dance program.

"Here, let me see that." Scanning it quickly, he whispered, "I'll be back," as he calmly erased three names and wrote in his own.

"Tom Huggins! What in the world are you doing?"

"Don't worry, Nancy. It is all arranged. One of those was your father, and the others—well, a little maneuvering here and there. Anyway, I want to talk to you. If I remember right, there is a bench in the garden—."

During his next turn, Tom skillfully danced me across the floor and out the French doors, and with his hand under my elbow, he guided me to a wrought iron bench in the shadow of a heavy-scented gardenia bush.

"Now Tom, You want to argue with me about marrying you and settling down in that lovely home of yours, but—"

"Yes, Nancy, I do. Our wise parents taught us that young folks should know each other's habits, build common interests, and a mental and spiritual companionship before they experiment much with the emotions. But you and I have known each other all of our lives. I don't remember how long we have been planning to marry, but we never got around to when. Now you have gotten all these restless ideas and you want to go traipsing away off to Galveston in search of adventure. Well, it's time you know my heart." He quickly gathered me into his arms and kissed me with a kiss that held his whole devotion. Fiery and independent, I flashed indignant, but a current flowed between us that melted my resistance. Fire and ice flowed through my veins and the night and the world stood still. Stunned by my first kiss, I quietly laid my head on Tom's shoulder. He whispered, "Nancy, my darling, I would wait for you forever, but I couldn't have you make a mistake about us. We were born for each other. We belong. You are mine!" His right arm tightened around me. "And I couldn't take a chance on losing you. All this Galveston business–Oh, Nancy! If anything should happen to you!" Tom shuddered. "I can't even bear to think about it. You're so gentle and sweet. You have no idea of what you might encounter. Your life has taught you to see good in everybody, but Nancy there are those who would trade on your gentle innocence. Some would see in your friendliness a weakness they can take advantage of." He drew me close to him. I turned swiftly, lifted my face and caught my breath.

"Oh, Tom—kiss me again." My voice was slightly more than a whisper. Tom looked at me soberly.

"We have a lifetime before us to express our love. But Nancy," he added as he slipped my hand over his pounding heart, "You are my heart, my life, my ideal. I was born for your service and protection. I shall make life good for you. I will be a proud man as I have you beside me. Oh Nancy, how gladly will I cherish, protect, and provide for you, my little darling, so long as God lets us live!" Passionately, he kissed me again. "Forget Galveston—don't go, Nancy. Let's go back in there and announce our wedding date. And oh darling, make it soon!" Tom trembled with the intensity of his emotions. I stubbornly pushed away.

"I am going. I'm going to Galveston if it's the last thing I ever do."

"Then, I'm going, too."

"No! You are not. And don't you dare follow me either! I'll never forgive you if you do. Promise you wont." "Very well, Little Miss Fancy." Tom smiled ruefully as he applied this term of endearment Poppa and I used for mother in times of disagreement and acquiescing.

"But it WILL be the last thing you do before you marry me. I serve notice here and now. As soon as you come back—" A chill thought struck him. "Nancy, you will come back?" I pressed my fingertips to lips still tingling from his kiss, and teased,

"Well, after that kiss I think—yes—you needn't worry. I'll be back."

Tom drew me to my feet, wrapped his long arms around me and kissed me again, thoroughly. Then, laughing exultantly, he let me go.

"My goodness, Tom! How am I going to go back in there and face all those people with all these skyrockets going off inside of me? And you, Tom—your face is lit up like a Christmas tree. The governor would take one look and say, "What hit him? A locomotive?" And Poppa and Miss Fancy? They've been married a long time, but I know how they look sometimes and I wager they wouldn't need two guesses."

"Whew! You're right, Nancy. But how do you expect a man not to be 'lit up' when he's positively drunk with happiness? Maybe if you go in this way, and I come around from the other side, perhaps we won't be so conspicuous if taken one at a time."

Chapter 8

Galveston : Late August, 1900.

I dozed to the rhythmic click-clacking of the train's wheels. For hours we had traveled across country that seemed incredibly flat to a girl accustomed to the hills and forests of Mississippi. Finally, we crossed into Texas. Our route skirted Houston, but since I could see for miles, its amazing skyline was clearly visible. Now at last, we neared Galveston. We approached the island city on a bridge nearly two miles long. Placid waters stretched out on either side below the train. The Conductor came through and called in his deep southern voice, "Gal-ves-ton. Next stop. All out . . . end of the line!" Viney and I hurried to gather our things. I could hardly wait for my first glimpse of the city and its gleaming sands stretching out to the sea.

Captain Hand himself, waited for me at the station. He had made arrangement for my trunk to be delivered.

"Welcome, Miss Nancy. We are so glad to have you come for a visit. I trust your journey went well." Offering his arm, he led me out to . . . a shining new yellow Oldsmobile motor car! Fearing I might appear a "country bumpkin," I focused on greeting Captain Hand and said nothing to reveal I had never ridden in an automobile before. He helped me into a cloak-like duster, seated me in the front passenger seat with Viney in the back, and away we went. Whizzing past horse-drawn carriages, barking dogs, and staring children at nearly ten miles an hour, it seemed we were flying. Meeting a bright silver Stanley Steamer, I resisted closing my eyes, but gripped the door, and braced myself, sure I was about to die. It honked its horn. "Ah-oooo-gah!" Passing us on the left, the other driver waved and steamed merrily on his way. I was breathless by the time we arrived at the Hand's home.

As the Captain neared his residence, he proudly explained, "We call our home, 'The Fort.' When Grace and I came to Galveston, we loved the ocean, its music, and the ever changing vista of sky and sea. We did not want to build back from the beach on the higher ridges as most people did. Instead, I shipped in boatloads of rich soil and reinforced it with deep steel pylons. We had a great terrace of masonry and earth built on the eastern tip of the island and upon that terrace, we built a wall, reinforced with masonry so that any high water would meet its match. From this perspective our residence draws its name. 'The Fort' sounds a bit forbidding, and the effect from the beach drive below is slightly grim. However, we are very happy with our modest estate."

To Viney and me, land-locked Mississippians, The Fort was magnificent. Inside the grounds, the brick walls were hidden by shrubs selected for their beauty from all parts of the world. Scarlet flowered hibiscus, pale ivory magnolia, white bridal wreath and shell pink crepe myrtle, alternated with multicolored oleanders. Here and there, a long leaf pine from the Captain's native Mississippi provided shade. One part of the grounds was devoted to an extensive formal rose garden. In this climate, roses prospered, blooming in December as well as May. The fragrant garden boasted lacy, wrought iron benches inviting one to rest and relax.

Lush grass covered the lawns on this unnatural promontory. Rich loam brought in from the Delta of the Mississippi River and almost daily rain showers provided excellent growing conditions for Captain and Mrs. Hand to plant to their hearts content. In the formal garden, there was a handcrafted sundial as well as a fountain. A marble cherub in the center of the fountain tirelessly trickled water from a large pink conch shell into a larger, shell-shaped basin, and finally into a large, free-form pond where large koi goldfish swam among lovely water lilies.

I stepped from the car and stared in spite of myself, speechless for the moment. The large round house, built round to deflect wind, was unlike any I had ever seen. It enchanted me. The first story was red brick. The upper stories were covered with cedar shingles weathered to a pale grey. balconies curved around on all three levels. Each balcony had an ornate, ironwork railing. Great white pillars rose from the ground, balcony to balcony in an unbroken line. A red tiled roof, cone shaped and steeply pitched completed "The Fort." The picture of Rapunzel's castle in my childhood storybooks came to my mind. I could hardly wait to see inside.

As I would learn later, Captain Hand's retreat occupied the topmost level of the house. His office walls were lined with treasures brought by his trade schooners from all over the world. Tall windows spanned the whole balcony of the third floor. The Hand twins called their father's domain, "The Crow's Nest," because he delighted in sitting there with his spyglass, identifying his ships as they passed back and forth from the harbor. He also kept a mounted telescope and studied the stars. Mrs. Hand sedately referred to this room as "The Observatory."

We arrived near noon. After a leisurely luncheon, and luxurious bath, I was glad to sit in the gardens for a quiet visit with Mrs. Hand. While we visited, she embroidered an organdy evening cape with incredibly fine stitches.

"Please call me 'Aunt Grace,' dear. Mrs. Hand sounds so formal, and your mother is as dear as a sister to me. Tell me about the folks back home, Nancy. I was raised in your community, you know, and growing up, your mother was my best friend. We had such happy times together. It was sweet of her to let us have you for a visit, but I do wish she could have come also." *I could hardly explain that I hadn't wanted mother to come. I had protested rebelliously about Viney, but finally gave in, when I found it was the price of Poppa's consent for my trip.*

Prompted by an occasional interested question from Aunt Grace, I recounted some news of the friends and neighbors "back home" in Clear Creek, Mississippi. "Do you remember the Lofton family? They have seven children now. They came to have Sunday dinner and visit with us, week before last. Their son, Wayne, recently felt called to the ministry. The Clear Creek Church probably hasn't changed much since you grew up there, except for an occasional new pastor. Brother Armes has been our pastor most of my life. He is a fine pastor and I just love his wife. She is my Sunday School teacher." Aunt Grace in turn regaled me with events of her childhood and college life where she and my mother were best friends and roommates. An hour passed quickly.

I wandered over and watched the fish swimming lazily in the pond. Excitement growing within made me want to leap to my feet, dance like a sprite, and sing like I had never sung before. *What is it?* I finally decided it was a combination of this fantasy-like garden, warm sunshine, whisper of the fountain, and the surging music of the wind and sea. It seeped into me, filling my mind and heart. I laughed out loud as I thought of what the locals hurrying by on the beach-road would think, if on the high buttress of "The Fort," a girl should suddenly burst into song.

Aunt Grace looked at me with inquiring eyes.

"It's just happiness bubbling over, I suppose—Oh, Aunt Grace, your home is like something out of a dream. This wall—I touched a lovely pink conch shell—the fountain— the sunshine— that balcony, like a stairway to the stars—the smell of the sea! It is all so enchanting. I feel I am walking in a dream!" Aunt Grace was familiar with the mesmerizing effect these things had on one who was new to them.

"I know just how you feel, dear. Take a deep breath. This atmosphere fills one's senses and can be overwhelming until one grows accustomed to it. You no doubt need an outlet for so much emotion." She turned to her nearly sixteen-year-old twins who had quietly joined us.

"Henrietta, a good set of tennis will be just the thing and then a dip in the ocean will give you all an appetite for dinner. But mind, I want Nancy back for the ' Magic Moment.' You understand."

"Magic Moment? What does she mean?"

"Oh, you'll see, Mother is an incurable romantic," Henry answered, and grinned at me.

"I think Mississippians are all half-breeds. Half romance and half poetry with a dash of prudery thrown in," added

Henrietta, swishing her tennis racket against the flowers. The intensity which crept into Henrietta's words surprised me.

"I didn't mean to be rude, Nancy. Come on, let's play!"

The tennis courts were on the side of the house away from the sea, on a level lower than the house. Giant oaks transplanted from their native soil in Louisiana at staggering cost and coaxed to grow here, shaded the courts. Sunburn was dangerous and a fine textured, fair skin was thought to be essential for ladies. Many men were also fair and nearly always wore long sleeves and straw hats. Fast matches ensued, first with Henry, then with Henrietta, after which we returned to the house to prepare for a swim.

"Here, Nancy, we are about the same size. This should fit you." Henrietta offered a blue sateen swimsuit, with a sailor collar and white braid trim. It was like a little dress reaching just to the knees, with bloomers and stockings to match. Beach shoes and a long cape were of the same material. After donning the ensemble, I saw my reflection in the mirror. The thought of appearing in public, in a garment showing my knees embarrassed me, but remembering Henrietta's remark about prudery, I determined not to show my concern. Etta's swimsuit was the just like mine except its buttercup yellow gave startling contrast to Etta's carrot colored hair. At the edge of the garden, we were met by Henry, attired in a suit that looked like my father's underwear, except for the wide blue and white stripes that chased each other around the loose shirt and tight fitting breeches. It was startling to me. I had never seen a man so nearly undressed. Henry caught the shock in my eyes and my blush as I hastily looked away.

"Slight shock to a Mississippi 'hillbilly'?" He chuckled, "Unaccustomed as they are to sea-shore *undress*."

"Not at all," I protested, but the tattle-tale blush still staining my cheeks gave me away.

"I was just admiring the barber-pole effect of the stripes." Henry laughed with good humor. His sister, always restless cried, "Race you! Last one in the water is a rotten-egg!" Laughing, all three of us ran down the stairs for my first dip in the sea.

"Oh! This is wonderful! To be part of this great, moving ocean." I discovered to my surprise that the water buoyed me up so that I could hardly sink. However, it is much more difficult to swim than it is in the cold, clear currents of the fresh-water streams at home. It seemed to me we had hardly begun to play when Henrietta touched her brother on the arm.

"Time to get Nancy home for the 'Magic Moment,' or Mother will be disappointed."

"Nancy would be, too, I imagine. So let's go. Tomorrow, Nancy, I'll teach you to ride the waves."

"But we have only been here a little while".

"About two hours, I imagine," Henry laughed again.

"You will learn that on the edge of the ageless ocean, our puny thing called time seems to stand still."

"Well, you are something of a poet, I would say!" He was always so goodnatured, it was a pleasure to be around him. "Oh, yes," he replied, smiling diffidently. "I do get romantic once in awhile. I am Mississippi-once-removed you know."

"Mississippi-removed-to-the-seashore. That is quite nice. In fact, lovely!" I linked arms with one twin on each side.

"Well, if we must, let's go."

Chapter 9 – Magic Moment

Henrietta supplied towels. "Do hurry Nancy. Wear something light and cool for dinner and get into it quickly. The 'Magic Moment' is only a moment indeed, and the whole family will be waiting in the Crow's Nest. I'll be back in just a minute. Be ready, if we miss it, Mother will have a fit!" She was gone before I could ask questions—*I thought about the undercurrent of bitterness in Henrietta's speech. It was almost as if she resented her mother's sweet sentimentality, but I found Aunt Grace charming.* I didn't want to rush–felt languorous. It was as if the sunlight and warm seawater had seeped into my bones. I just wanted to stretch and dream, but mindful of 'Etta's caution, I quickly rinsed off the salt water, allowed Viney to dry me briskly and hurried into my dainty lace trimmed under garments, including full petticoats. Quickly, Viney slipped the cool sprigged muslin gown over my head. It was made for general wear, but hinted at formal, with its round embroidered yoke, ruffled sleeves and skirt. Handmade lace trimmed the bodice and sleeves and edged the ruffles. A wide black, velvet sash and patent leather slippers completed my ensemble.

"Hurry, Viney. Whatever the 'Magic Moment's is, I want

you to see it, too." Before the older woman could question, Etta reappeared,

"Can Viney come also?" "Of course. Mother says she is like one of the family anyway. She can share our "Magic Moment," but we had better hurry or we'll miss it." Chattering, we hurried to climb the short flight of stairs to the crow's nest. Viney, huffing and puffing brought up the rear. One whole side of "the Crow's Nest" was thrown open to the late afternoon sunlight. My host and hostess sat on the balcony, smiling in anticipation.

"Well here we are. Please tell me what this "Magic Moment" is? I'm consumed with curiosity."

"Just wait, my dear. When night falls, then you will see it. We have no twilight here, one minute it is day, then, night comes, but for just a moment between them . . . you shall see. Stand over there by the banister where you can watch the sea and the sky." Captain placed a wicker chair with a fluffy cushion next to the balcony for Viney. All fell silent, waiting for the coming of the mystic spell. Motionless, I stood by the banister. I felt the nostalgia of late evening and thought of the day-closing sounds on the plantation. Here on the island, one moment the sunlight was bright on land and sea, then suddenly it dimmed as if some giant hand had been placed over the sun. Almost mystically the landscape—ocean and the air itself were silver! For a moment the elements all seemed one—like mist or a soft chiffon curtain one could touch with a hand.

"The Magic Moment." Then swift as a breath, night came.

Permeating my being was the magic of this wide sky, these people, their man-made paradise. It all seemed one with the eternal God-given mystery of the sea. Exaltation had been building up in me all day. It overflowed and I found myself singing, softly at first and then pouring out song. High and clear as crystal, my joyous expression swept out into the vast night. From the beach below, came applause. I was appalled by my outburst. I ran to Viney and tucking my face into her familiar shoulder, I burst into tears.

"Marvelous!" whispered Aunt Grace, clapping. "Wonderful!" echoed Captain Hand. "The most remarkable performance I have ever heard! Nancy, I had no idea you had such a voice. This moment of magic has always seemed so beautiful to me. Now I shall forever think of your music completing it when our silvery twilight falls."

"I am so sorry! What must you think of me, I forgot myself completely. We are so isolated at home, I have fallen into the habit of singing whenever the notion strikes me, and this has been building up inside me all day. This lovely home, my first glimpse of the sea, you kind friends and now this wonderful Magic Moment—The music simply escaped me. Those people on the beach must think you have a lunatic locked up in The Fort. I think the wind is partly to blame. Ever since I arrived it has been blowing, and blowing."

"You will get used to it," Henry sought to reassure me. "It blows like that all the time."

"I wonder if I will, it exhilarates me greatly—like music in my veins." Captain Hand laughed. "You are quite the most charming thing in captivity, Miss Nancy. And such talent! You should have an audition with Schuman Heink, the great vocal director of the Metropolitan Opera House in New York. That voice belongs to the world."

"Don't be embarrassed, Nancy." Aunt Grace said. "You have given us pleasure we shall not forget. But now, let's have our dinner, and then we want you to sing for us again. Your voice truly is remarkable."

Etta silently thought, Huh! If I could sing like that, everyone would pay attention to me. Though she thought "everyone," she had a one particular one in mind. After a moment, Etta linked her arm with mine and we descended the stairs. Henry courteously gave his arm to Viney. I thought I detected some real heartache in Etta, and wondered what was troubling my new friend, only fifteen years old.

Chapter 10 – The Tour

Morning came softly in the castle by the sea. I was first
conscious of sound, as usual. Not the familiar morning sounds
of the plantation but the constant wind and the deep rolling
whisper of the sea. I thought briefly of my mockingbird friend
at home, but this was a different kind of singing. Puzzled by my
inner reaction, I lay listening and a melody began to sing inside
me— forming itself, taking shape as I listened. I could hear
it clearly in my mind, just as if remembering a familiar tune.

"Good morning, sweet chile. Is you gonna sleep this day
away?" Viney teased as usual while she poured hot water into
the pretty china washbowl. She helped me bathe and dress and
we joined the family for breakfast. Even though I chatted with
the family, in the back of my mind, the new melody persisted.

"Nancy dear, the twins are going into town to do the
marketing for me. Would you like to go along?"

"I believe, Aunt Grace," I touched her affectionately on the
hand, "I prefer to remain here. I have letters I must write."

"To your mother and to that nice Huggins boy, I imagine.
Well, give your mother my love and tell her we are enjoying
her lovely daughter very much. Tell her, also, that we would

be most happy if she and your father should find it possible to join us. Perhaps though, I shall find time to write to her myself this evening. You will find books and magazines in the library, and the view from the observatory is always interesting. I trust you will not be lonely. Call me if there is anything you desire."

"I am sure I will not be lonely in this beautiful place. I will get my letters finished and then just roam around the garden if you don't mind."

"Not at all, dear. Make yourself at home. I must get these children off with my grocery list. I will see you later, and if you want anything just pull the call bell."

Left alone, I stood looking out across the balcony and the garden, conscious every moment of the wind and the sea. I wandered about the room, picking up a book, fingering a bit of bric-a-brac, finally drifting into the drawing room where I stood by the window and fell into reverie. How long I stood there I have no idea, thinking of the home folks one at a time... Sally and the others, and, of course, Tom.

Dear sweet Tom, I know I love him, but whether I will ever go back or not, I just don't know. When I think of the slow, even pace of our life in Mississippi, and contrast it with the fairy tale like atmosphere and beauty of this place—the warm rays of the sun and serenade of the wind and sea—.They just seem to take possession of me. They becomes part of the music I've been hearing in my mind all morning. As if drawn, I sat at the baby grand piano and struck an experimental chord—a low booming one. I repeated it softly three times, then struck an octave and a single. As if recalling a familiar melody, music flowed from my mind and fingers. First, the low soft "boom", then the echoing chords in ascending octaves like the curving lips of the waves. Again the long slow roll, and the repeating pattern reaching upward like the waves rolling in from the sea. Again and again, with ever recurring "boom—roll," imitating the ceaseless waves. Suddenly, with both hands in the treble, I began to play a running melody, light and shallow like the stretch of calm water before the edge of the sea whispers over the sand—a sparkling, lilting melody like the shallows where children play. Then back out to sea with new rollers gathering. Again that boom—roll—roll! Surprised and delighted, I dropped my hands from the keys.

There, in the doorway, stood the Captain and Mrs. Hand. Smiling and applauding they came into the room.

"Nancy, that was amazing! I'm so glad that Mr. Hand dropped by in time to hear it. He is quite a lover of good music." Then, looking puzzled, she asked,

"But what is it? I play quite a wide variety but have never heard—"

"It is like the rolling of the ocean," exclaimed Mr. Hand. "I am sure I would not have forgotten if I had ever heard it before. What is it, Nancy?"

"I don't know." I shrugged my shoulders. "I've been hearing it in my mind all morning. The winds and the waters becoming music—I suppose I would call it 'The Majesty of The Sea.'"

"Your own composition? My dear, that was wonderful. You must let me help you get it on paper—you must not lose it." Turning to his wife, my host smiled.

"This visitor proves full of unexpected pleasures." He patted me on the back. "Her parents won't like it but I think we'll have to keep Miss Nancy here." I smiled at him.

"I love it here by this beautiful sea!"

"Yes, the ocean is beautiful—but fickle. It can be very dangerous as well."

The commotion of the twins returning interrupted. As they came in, Henrietta said to her brother, "Here, Henry, you take all these things to the kitchen," and to her Mother, "Here are your stamps and handkerchiefs. Are they what you wanted?" Turning to me, she exclaimed,

"Oh, Nancy, I can't wait to take you to Garden Verien. It is a gorgeous place, and you will meet all our good friends there."

"Whoa, slow down, Etta, catch a breath," her mother told her with a chuckle.

"It is courteous to have your friends meet your guests in your own home, first. We will arrange a party here for tomorrow evening and take Nancy to the Garden Friday night. Help me get the lists made out. While you two show Nancy the city, I will communicate the invitations to our guests. Many of them are already expecting it, so we will encounter no difficulties, even though the time is short.

A dinner party first, then dancing and charades later, don't you think?"

"Yes, mother—but does it have to be so old-fashioned?" Father looked at her sharply, but said nothing. Mother said only, "Henrietta . . ."

Early that afternoon, we three young people set out in the Oldsmobile for a tour of the city. The twins took turns driving. They honked the horn and waved merrily to their friends as we sped along. I flinched when the automobile frightened a horse, and it reared, almost unseating its rider. The Oldsmobile and its merry trio seemed to attract attention everywhere we went. Henry and each of us girls wore linen dusters, or light coats, to protect our clothes. Etta, as she was often called, and I also wore broad-brimmed sun hats tied on our heads with long silk scarves, which blew out like streamers behind us. As

I became more accustomed to our speed, I thought, *I could never get enough of this semi-tropical city. Its divided streets, called boulevards, with riots of colorful flowers and green palm trees growing down the center are amazing.*

Henry was a good tour guide. He explained, "The founding fathers laid out this city for beauty and permanence. There are wide avenues north and south and seventy foot wide streets. Two great boulevards bisect the island. One of these, Broadway, is one hundred fifty feet wide. The flowered bushes growing down the center of it are called oleanders. The other boulevard, Bath, runs at right angles to Broadway. It is one hundred twenty feet wide, and also has an esplanade with oleanders and palms. The blocks are uniformly laid out, two hundred sixty by three hundred feet." To Nancy, accustomed to thinking in acres and miles, this did not mean much but the gracious palm-lined boulevards amazed her. With their crushed white oystershell paving, they provided perfect background for the fantastic tropical palms and flowers.

Etta pointed out stately and elaborate dwellings and explained, "There are restrictions against building inferior houses." Driving along the harbor, Henry fired my imagination as he identified multitudes of foreign ships by their flags. With pride, he took us to his father's own docks where dockhands and seafarers alike smiled as they greeted the boss's redheaded twins. The tour continued. Henrietta put in proudly, "This island is barely two miles wide, but we have our own churches, a business district, hospital and schools."

I was spellbound as we rode the ferry and watched the dolphins at play all around the moving boat. For this central Mississippi girl, Bolivar Lighthouse, its height and its purpose, as explained by the twins, was another wonder. The grand finale of our tour was a drive down the gleaming white sands of the beach. Henrietta pointed out Murdoch's Beach house and the great oriental bathing pavilion known as the Pagoda. When we passed the grand resort, Olympia, Etta identified it, with its Club Verien, and its tropical bower. She proudly announced, "The cream of Galveston Society congregates here, and this is where we will party this weekend—in costume!" Henrietta seemed thrilled at the prospect of the party there, and her excitement infected me, too, when she said it was to be a costume affair.

"I brought the perfect costume. I can wear Great Aunt Nancy's antique ball gown, with all its accessories. I'm so glad it is to be in costume!"

"So am I. But just wait until you meet —"A disapproving look from her brother stopped her from finishing the sentence. Etta became sulky. Little more was said until we reached The Fort, where our tired trio was just in time for supper.

Chapter 11 – Surprises

Surrounded by elegance, silver, lace, crystal, candlelight, laughter and congenial conversation, dinner was delightful. A variety of perfectly prepared seafood, fresh from the gulf waters made a feast fit for a king. Key Lime pie completed the delightful meal. These delicious foods were all new to me, but I enjoyed them thoroughly. Captain Hand and Aunt Grace were excellent hosts and skillfully included both their mature and younger guests in stimulating conversation. After dinner, everyone moved to the living room where Mrs. Hand played the piano and we all joined in singing popular music as well as folk songs. Several of the young guests had brought instruments and joined in the accompaniment. To me it seemed strange that so many of the young people openly held hands and embraced each other. *I'm a stranger here and not accustomed to this liberty, but I must not judge.* After a while, Aunt Grace stood and surprised me by asking,

"Nancy, would you share your new composition with us?" I blushed and seated myself at the piano. "I am still working out the details, but it is called 'The Majesty of the Sea." I played, and everyone seemed fascinated, but Henrietta broke the spell saying,

"Very pretty. Our Nancy is a lady of many talents. Next, father will want her to sing, but let's go out to the garden for that." Complimenting me and applauding, the young people moved into the garden. A young man caught me by the hand. It startled me but not wanting to embarrass him, or myself, I said nothing.

Aunt Grace placed an arm about my shoulders and said to the young man, "Please excuse us for a moment." Leading me a few feet away, she said sympathetically, "Our young people may surprise you. They are casual in some ways I do not approve, but I seem unable to change that. A seaport town may be beautiful but it certainly cultivates a casual culture among its people." At that moment, the Captain came, took his wife's hand, and coaxed, "Come dear, our adult guests are waiting in the parlor." I joined the young people outside.

The garden took on an ethereal beauty in the bright moonlight. I observed young couples on benches and some reclining on the ground in various degrees of embrace. Henrietta, waited for me with two young men. She held a mandolin under her arm. One young man held a violin and the other a beautiful black guitar. "Sit over here and sing. We will accompany you," she invited. "But what shall I sing?" The violinist, adjusted his beautifully polished instrument under his chin, drew a soft note, and skillfully began to play a popular tune. I joined with the others singing, but the strangeness of the scene disturbed me. No one else seemed to notice. To me, it seemed the music had no real importance for them. It was merely a background for their moonlight passions. My parents always urged, "Hands off and talk it out." It didn't seem that advice had reached here. For a time we sang, first one song and then another. Finally Etta, her eyes gleaming, laid down her

62

mandolin. A look passed between her and violin player and together they slipped away. Across the garden they sank down, locked tight in each other's arms.

The guitar player introduced himself to me. "My name is Joe Evans, Nancy, and that leaves just us. What are we going to do about it?" That was indeed a huge question. The garden was almost silent. Here a whisper, there a giggle, a caught breath or a sigh. To me it was incredible the way these young people played so freely at love. Joe slipped his arm around me as we stepped in front of a bench. "I think I prefer to sit here," I said and slipped from his arm and onto the bench.

Okay, he thought, hard to get is her game. He sat on the ground, locked his arms around his knees, leaned back against the bench and requested, "Well, tell me about Mississippi."

I am usually good at conversation and easy laughter, but found conversation awkward in this amorous, moonlit atmosphere. At first, Joe gave me no help, but I persisted, asking questions about his interests, and soon had him laughing and inquiring about my favorite activities at home. As we talked, his shoulder and dark curly head came to rest against my knee. This made me uneasy, but I did not want to embarrass him, or myself, so I ignored the unwanted physical contact. In the quiet, it seemed to me I was chattering like a magpie. Strange—I had never felt myself so nervous before. I expected to be able to carry on an interesting conversation with anyone, young or old. I had always been friendly toward everyone, with a ready laugh and a quick repartee, but in the middle of a conversation about horses, a thought burst into my mind, *"Fun." This isn't any fun—this experimenting with emotions. Where had I heard that? Tom! I wish he was here now.*

Turning, Joe laid his arm across my knees and placed his

chin on it, regarding me with an inviting gleam in his eyes. "Come on. Let's take a stroll around the garden. Those lips were made for kissing." He stood and drew me to my feet, linked his arm through mine and clasped my hand tightly. Our stroll took us toward the shadow of the balcony's edge. Suddenly, I stumbled.

"OH, my ankle! Let's sit down here for a moment." Grimacing, I tentatively wiggled my foot. "Is it bad? Should I call Etta?"

"No, don't disturb the others. Just help me into the house and I will call my mammy, Viney, to doctor it for me."

"Your *mother's* here?" he exclaimed!

"No, No. Viney is my servant, but much more so, my friend. She has been with me my whole life. I assure you she is very capable."

Joe assisted me into the living room, seated me on the couch and placed several cushions under the injured foot.

"Are you sure there is nothing more I can do for you. I 'm sorry you hurt your foot."

"Thank you, Joe, for your thoughtfulness. I apologize for my clumsiness. There is no need for you to miss the rest of the party." I insisted he rejoin the others. "When Etta misses me just tell her I have retired. She can drop in after all her guests have gone, if she wishes."

Protesting and expressing desire for my comfort, Joe finally returned to the garden. I slipped out on the dark balcony which overlooked the garden below, just in time to see him sit down by a couple in front of an oleander bush and add his arm to the one already snuggling the girl's waist.

"Room for one more?"

"Oh, hello honey," the girl murmured. "Lonesome?" She

laughed and kissed one boy and then the other. Long, lingering kisses. I shuddered and thought of Tom's kiss—of the long years of devotion that had gone before it and of the deep meaning it held. I was aghast at this public and casual exchange of caresses. As if in answer to my thoughts, I heard a male voice below the balcony.

"Etta," he was saying, intensely, "Let's get married!"

"Married? What a crazy idea. You're seventeen years old and I'm not even sixteen yet!

"I know we're young, but I love you. I mean, *really love you*, and I want to marry you. I want to really love you forever. This "playing around" isn't good enough for you and you won't even say you love me."

"I love this," Etta giggled and an interval of silence followed.

"I love it, too Etta, God help me, but my love for you goes deeper than this. I love you like a man ought to love his wife, with tenderness and respect. It sickens me to play around like this with you, feeling the way I do. I want to offer you a real love that is right and permanent. I want to make a home for you and protect you. I want to work for you, but all you want is— Etta, if you don't love me how can you —"

"Too much talk—." Etta giggled.

I went up to bed.

Chapter 12 – After the Party

Tuesday dawned clear and balmy. For once, no sea wind was blowing. I missed it immediately. Very late last night, Henrietta had tapped gently on my door. Henry came as far as the door, but withdrew after being informed that my accident was slight. Etta turned her face away and twitched at her skirts impatiently.

"I hope the party was not *too* grim. I apologize for not coming sooner. I didn't even know you had gone. I didn't miss you actually, I was busy." I laughed.

"I should say you were! Nice lad, that Willard, and all yours, it seems."

"Oh, he's alright, but too serious."

"Why Etta, I thought you liked him."

"I do like him. I'm crazy about him in a way, but he is such a baby. I've known him all my life—not my idea of romance at all. Sometimes I can put up with him, but when he gets so deadly serious, I almost can't stand him."

Why Etta, if you feel that way?"

"I know—Miss Mississippi-touch-me-not, just like Mother. Well a girl has to have some fun." I was silent, partly from embarrassment, partly because I was at a loss for what to say. I had never considered myself prudish, but simply could not imagine such casual physical contact. It certainly didn't match my idea of party fun. Instead, a grim seriousness had seemed to settle over the garden, like compulsion. If the twins were any example, they evidently had not enjoyed the party much either.

"Did you really have fun?" I asked gently, ignoring Etta's rudeness. For a moment, she just looked at me. Then to my surprise, she sat on the floor, tucked her face down on her knees and said on a shuddering breath,

"Oh, Nancy I'm so sorry I was rude to you, but I admire you, and I just hate myself. I don't know what comes over me, I didn't really have fun, but everybody else does it, and I want to be like them. Afterward, when I am alone I feel sick and ashamed. Nancy, I feel torn in two. When I look at Mother and Father, such fine people, I feel shoddy and cheap and yet I probably wouldn't act any different even if I could. Why can't I just be like some of the other girls. It doesn't seem to bother them." Etta looked at me, with tears and a troubled expression. She shook her head as if to clear her thoughts.

"Well, I certainly seem to be anything but happy." She seemed on the point of saying something else but hesitated then, "Anyway, I'm glad you weren't really hurt." Resuming her usual sarcastic tone, "Don't worry about me. I'll be okay." With a quick wave from the doorway, she was gone.

I slid under the covers, but my mind at work on this conversation and the one I had overheard, convinced me something in Henrietta's nature predicted real trouble for this child. Whose influence was spoiling her young life? What could an outsider like me do to help? I prayed for her, that God would open her eyes and heart, and asked God for wisdom for her sweet parents, myself, and for some opportunity making it possible to help Etta—something that would bring true happiness and peace to her.

Chapter 13 – An Invitation

Early the next morning, Henrietta knocked on my door, so excited, she rushed in without waiting for me to invite her in. "I can hardly wait. This noon we are lunching at Garden Verein. Be sure to wear your best outfit. You are going to love this place. It is a fiesta of flowers and colors and sound, and the people..." Etta fluttered her eyes. Suddenly, as if she just realized what she had done, "Oh Nancy, I'm sorry I just burst into your room like this. I am so excited, I forgot my manners. Please excuse me. I will leave, so you can get ready."

Remembering Etta's chatter about the exclusiveness of this club, I chose a suit in muted blue, just a shade less blue than my eyes. A fine wide silk frill lined the open cuffs and filled in the low neck and bodice. My tight fitting jacket had a short flared peplum. A long gored skirt, gray kid leather shoes with pointed toes, and white gloves completed my ensemble. When almost ready to depart for the club, I donned my gray satin hat, similar to a small derby, rolled back a little on each side of the brim. Where it tilted across my left eye, a blue and green bird made of exotic feathers perched as if looking down at the wearer. Etta approved.

When we arrived at The Garden Verien, the Concierge greeted the Hands by name, and escorted us to their reserved table. Here and there, parties from all about the country, were seated over seafood and wine. From the number of young men present, I suspected my hosts had done some discreet planning, for most of these were older than Henrietta and Henry's crowd. Progressing through the room, we paused here and there for introductions and greetings.

As we approached the far end of this lovely solarium, a bright green macaw on a golden perch greeted us loudly, "Hellooo, Beautiful!" He ruffled his feathers, and strutted.

When our party arrived at our reserved tables, the Captain introduced me to guests from Austin, Lake Charles, Dallas, and San Antonio as well as some local friends. I was slightly embarrassed to recognize Joe Evans, from last night's party, but he winked at me with good nature, as if to let me know he had not been fooled by my "sprained ankle" ploy.

This is it, these are the kinds of friends I have been seeking— sophisticated, charming and alive. Oh, I am going to enjoy this visit. One of the handsome young men seated me. My neighbor on the right, Suellen McCallen, a wealthy rancher's daughter, was admiring the antique pearl on my right hand when I caught a subtle gesture from Etta, toward a gentleman several tables away. The young man, realizing I saw them, smiled a provocative smile. Excusing himself from his companion, he made his way to our table. This man, different than any I had ever met, had a charming aura about him. He seemed suave, poised, and radiated charm. His slender face flared to high cheekbones. Slightly slanted eyes like brown velvet under arched brows accented the soft tan of his skin. A smile of incredible charisma played over even white teeth. His dimples ran into the flair of his cheeks and gave him a puckish sort of smile.

As he approached our table, his dignity seemed almost regal. Captain Hand rose from his seat and the visitor bowed to Mrs. Hand. "You will pardon this intrusion? I have met your children, the twins, and I hoped to have the pleasure . . ."

"Oh yes, Mother," Henrietta blurted, "This is Andre LeJuene. We met at the yacht club. He is from Louisiana. His boat is here." She regained her poise, "May I introduce my parents, Captain and Mrs. Hand."

"It is our pleasure to meet you," responded the Captain. "Won't you join us?"

"Thank you, no. You see I have a guest." He motioned toward his table. "But please return to your seat. This is indeed a pleasure," said LeJuene. "One I had not anticipated. On second thought, I shall sit down for a moment. Charlotte will excuse me that long."

"Shall I order something for you?"

"Thank you, but my lunch has already been served."

"LeJuene? The name is unusual. I am wondering if we know your people? asked Mrs. Hand.

"I doubt it, Madam. We are an old Arcadian family. My parents do not get out very much. They are contented with their quiet life among the moss hung oaks of our country."

"Let me see. 'LeJuene and Son Importers.' Any connection?" asked the Captain.

"Yes, sir. In fact my father is the 'Son'. I am Andre the third, and you must be 'Hand Import Company', correct?"

"Right again. I am well acquainted with your firm. Glad to know you. Won't you at least have something to drink?"

"No, thank you, I must return to my table, but before I

do, may I have the pleasure of inviting your party for a cruise on my boat, and dinner tomorrow night? To be followed by dancing, of course."

"I am sorry, but Mrs. Hand and I are otherwise engaged."

"But the young folks, they may come?"

Several spoke up eagerly. Captain and Mrs. Hand exchanged glances.

"We shall see, and will let you know as soon as possible, if that is acceptable to you, of course. Where may we reach you?"

"Quite satisfactory, and you may reach me at the Galvez. I trust the answer will be favorable. And now, if you will excuse me?" Etta was tense. To my surprise, I felt motion under the edge of the table as Etta squeezed LeJuene's hand. With perfect composure, the man leisurely returned to his own table. I was sure I was the only one aware of their gesture. I wondered about it, but turned my attention to my meal.

After dinner, the twins preferred to return home, but I rode to town with the adults, to do a little shopping.

"I do not like this, our children meeting strangers that way and bringing them into our circle. This man, 'LeJuene, do you know anything about him?"

"No, I only know his firm. They are Arcadian French, an old family. The original Andre was a Viscount, I have heard. There was a rumor that his father engaged in the slave trade, but the firm is respectable enough now. Substantial too, I imagine. In fact very wealthy."

"But this man. He is too smooth—too sophisticated for our children. I do not want them to go on that boat." Now I had been greatly attracted to Mr. LeJuene. He had vitality, was so poised and graceful. He likewise had an air of mischief, as if he were laughing at life behind all that polish and gentility.

His very differences fascinated me and fired my romantic imagination.

"He seemed quite nice to me. And if there are chaperones?"

"Henrietta protests so against chaperones. She seems to consider them a reflection on her character, rather than as a protection for her good name. Oh dear, I do fear this means trouble. We should have accepted ourselves and prevented this situation."

"Please excuse us, Nancy, discussing our problems before you. But we must come to a decision as to whether the children may go. There seems no way that we can ensure proper chaperones."

"If the cruise is to be afternoon and include an evening dinner, why not take Viney along to assist us with our dressing. She is as good a chaperone as you could want, and surely there would be no objection to that."

"The very thing. I know those Mississippi mammies. I had one, too, you know. That will solve the problem. I would hate to disappoint Etta. She thinks I am reactionary. I am afraid I will someday bring her to rebellion if I'm not careful."

She is in rebellion now but doesn't really know what she wants.

Chapter 14 – Aboard the White Swan

I tried not to gawk at the size of *The White Swan*. In such a yacht, one could sail the seas. The open spaces of the deck were canopied in striped awnings. Even the deep sea fishing deck was shaded by colorful canvas. The Swan's equipment included every luxury and convenience imaginable. A spacious dining salon, comfortable cabins, a polished dance floor... no sparing of money or good taste was apparent anywhere. The command came, "Up anchor!"

Instantly, the engine sounds changed. The yacht came about slowly, and put out through the harbor between the tip of the island and Bolivar Peninsula and, as LeJuene explained, "over the bar." The sky was clear and sunny with occasional puffs of wind. Seeing the vast stretch of water was a never-ending delight to this land-locked Mississippi girl. I had never before been on a craft larger than a rowboat! I could hardly contain my excitement when LeJuene pointed out the porpoises, rolling around the boat and playing like children. Later, he led me to the stern and showed me the chattering seagulls. It is amazing the way they sail on motionless, curving wings, rising, falling, gliding from side to side, seemingly without effort.

"How do they do that?"

My host explained, "They ride the currents where the boat has disturbed the air, much like one floats with the current on the fresh water streams of our country."

"Hmm. I never thought of the air having currents like water. I love to float. Just lie back with my hands behind my head and be carried along on the water."

"But the gull," LeJuene said, laughing, "must spread his wings, so that his feathers can catch the wind-drift. His soft rounding body is beautiful, too, against the summer air." *Somehow I felt he was imagining my body outlined against the water and the two-edged compliment embarrassed me.*

"Look! The water is becoming clear. Why, you can see the fish swimming and the water is like an artist's green water color."

"This ink could write a fascinating story, I imagine. It has been the pathway of pirates, explorers, and adventurers of every kind."

"What are those fish with umbrellas over their heads and pretty streamers hanging down?"

"There? Those are Portuguese Man Of War. They are pretty, but those colorful ribbons bear a very painful sting."

Joe spoke up, "A friend and I were fishing from stepladders we had set up on a sand bar. He stepped down to go back to the beach for more bait, and about halfway to shore, one of those things hit his leg. He instinctively slapped it off, and it wrapped around his other leg. He was screaming and thrashing around in the water. I didn't know what had happened or what to do. By the time I got him to the hospital emergency room, he had a fever and huge welts all up and down both legs where he had been stung. The doctor said the best first-aid would have been to immediately reach down, grab wet sand and scrub vigorously to remove as much venom as possible. I sincerely hope I never have occasion again to need that advice."

Our host assured us that the only fish on board the White Swan would be ones invited, (caught by us.) He continued identifying interesting things.

"Perhaps we shall see a sword fish. Watch that school of small fish scatter. The larger fish which plunged into their midst was a young hammerhead shark."

"Gee whiz, I thought sharks were much bigger. I wonder what happened to that shark's head? Looks like he ran head-on into a boat," quipped Kyle.

"That was a Hammer Head shark, so called for their flat heads. There are many kinds of sharks, and they come in all sizes...some grow as large as whales. However, we are unlikely to see one any larger than twenty feet long in the gulf." A long pause allowed time for expressions of shock, fear, anxiety, excitement, and finally disbelief to play on the faces of the young guests.

"Just teasing!" LeJuene's chuckle was joined first by tentative and then hearty laughs and relief all around.

"If any of you are interested, there is an extensive library containing information on sea life. It is on the lower deck and you are welcome to browse in it. Would anyone enjoy a try at deep sea fishing later this evening?"

"I should love it," said Suellen. "I am an avid fisherman. Father says I spend too much time fishing instead of ranching."

"I would like to take on one of those flat fish you pointed out—those Ling," said Kyle.

"Good. We will give fishing a try, when the sun cools a little. But come, let's walk over to the port side where everyone can get a view of the island."

We had been cruising in a southeasterly direction, which took us away from the island. There it lay to the north, like a child's toy stretched out on the ocean.

"Is that the island? Is that Galveston? It hardly seems higher than the water and seems so much larger when we are on it."

"Well, it isn't much higher than the water," LeJuene, who seemed to take great pleasure in my surprise, laughed. "Nor is it very big. The whole island is only 30 miles long, not much more than two miles wide at the widest point. And, it is only nine feet above sea level at high tide. Someday King Neptune may just reach up and erase it from the map."

I couldn't help shuddering. "Good gracious, you scare me. It seems large when we are on it."

"Yes," our host admonished, "Many things look different from a distance."

"They certainly do," I agreed. Our party approached the Skipper. He saluted and addressed LeJuene. "Somewhat unusual calm, sir, I have seldom seen the water so still. Color's a bit off, also. If we were in the Caribbean, the natives would say this foretold a typhoon. You know their saying, "The ocean gathers himself before he springs.""

"My goodness, I shall have the heebee-jeebees first thing you know. Mr. LeJuene tells us that Galveston lies low in the water, now you follow up with typhoons!" Both men laughed heartily. The Captain said, "Galveston does indeed lie close to the water. Some day a real storm could do fearful damage there. A tropical storm blows in a spiral, such as children learn when studying penmanship. The whorl sometimes reaches a hundred miles or more an hour as it progresses, doing terrible damage. The strange thing is, at the center of a hurricane, there is a core of absolute calm. It is called the eye of the storm. Should such a storm as is at present blowing up toward Florida, blow west along this coast and hit just right, Galveston would first feel the wind blowing from the North. In this hemisphere, the action is always counter-clock-wise from right to left at the top of the spiral. This would have the effect of sweeping the waters of the coastal area back to sea. Then, as the storm progresses, the bottom of the spiral would swing around in a tremendous tidal wave, and pour it out on the coast. In such a case, what the winds did not destroy, the wave would engulf and scatter like match-sticks across the plain."

I shivered again. "Goodness, I sure hope a storm like that will wait until I'm not here!"

The Captain laughed. "No need to worry. Galveston says that particular combination of elements will never hit here, because of the configuration of the coastline. The storm would turn northward before it hit the island, or south, so as to miss the island completely. Besides, the normal course of those storms is up the Atlantic seaboard. It would be without precedent for one to turn due west and proceed here. However, if one should ever hit just right, I profoundly hope that I am in other waters, far removed from this place."

"And I hope I am in my good old Mississippi hills where we only have simple storms with thunder and lightening once in a while." I laughed and the other guests laughed with me.

"That is a strange phenomena of these storms. They have no thunder or lightening, nor lowering clouds, just gray atmosphere and continuous winds that blow and blow ever harder, so that one accustomed to inland storms can hardly realize their dangerous nature. I have seen Mississippi storms. Grey, inky clouds advancing full of lightening and awesome claps of thunder until as the storm draws near, it sometimes has the sound of an approaching train. They are fearsome indeed, yet not to be compared with a hurricane, which does not threaten, but merely grows, until sometimes the buildings crumble in its grasp. It can also pile up waves that set seagoing vessels far inland and leave them there. Don't worry, a storm is hardly going to blow up out of this clear sky."

"Whew, I am really glad to hear that." I wasn't the only one who breathed a sigh of relief.

"And now, enough storm talk. Who wants to do some fishing?"

To the boat captain, LeJuene said as he turned away, "Keep an eye on the glass and let me hear from you if need be."

"Aye, aye, sir," said the Captain, saluting.

"Galveston," I said, my arms were crossed on the railing, "Playground of the North. City by the Sea. Fantasy Land, I call it, looking at it from here… City of My Dreams. I think I've been looking for it all my life and am just finding it. That probably sounds absurd to you." I laughed at myself.

"Not absurd, but interesting." LeJuene, nodded and grinned that charming grin, "This spot really is interesting. Once there were two islands with a deep pass between them. In the early 19th century, a storm closed the pass and made one long island of it."

"What? Why I never knew it had ever been anything but one lovely spot!" exclaimed Suellen.

"Yes," continued LeJuene, "And it has been many kinds of places in its history. In 1582 explorers were wrecked upon it. They called it Malhado, meaning misfortune. Cabesa de Vaca was captured by Indians. He escaped and returned to Spain. From his account it became Isla de Las Culebras, 'The Island of Snakes.' Later it was called San Louis in honor of a Spanish king. In 1785 its name honored Count Bernardeo de Galvez, Viceroy of Mexico. In 1816 it was claimed by Mexico and Don Louis Avery used it as a base for preying on Spanish vessels. Then later, he was joined by Francisco Xavior Mina and his two hundred men. Together they plotted raiding the Mexican coast but quarreled before they could do so."

"Around 1819, Louisiana drove Jean LaFitte and his pirates from their coast. They sailed into Galveston Bay and took possession of the Island. It was much to their liking and they renamed it 'Campechi'."

"Campechi." I laughed, "Evidently Camp Peachy. An apt sense of gaity at least."

"Oh, but you would not have liked their camp very well, I am afraid. Gradually the number of pirates grew to over a thousand. They began to import Indian squaws and Negro women. There was plenty of loot, and liquor flowed freely. A hodge-podge of dwelling places came into being. LaFitte, always the leader, began to assemble a home for himself. It gradually became a warehouse, a dwelling place and a fortress, with cannon on each corner of the upper story. He called it Maison Rouge, or the Red House. The village surrounding it contained gambling halls, saloons, and all sorts of places, including a slave market, where captured people, of all races and genders were sold as slaves. It is said slaves sold for a dollar a pound!"

"How horrible," I muttered.

"Exactly." LeJuene, enjoying the rapt attention of his young guests continued, "In 1818, Campechi reached its peak.

Privateers from all points of the compass came here. That year, two of the Napoleons' generals, L'Allemand and Rigand, along with four hundred adventurers of 'tough elegance' settled nearby, and court life sprung up, with Maison Rouge as its center." Nancy, looking at the water, made no comment, so LeJuene changed tactics. "Over a hundred Spanish ships were pirated. There was fighting by day and reveling by night. The United States considered cleaning the vile place out, but had to abandon action because Spain, the major victim, protested. In 1819, one of LaFitte's crew fired on a United States ship, against LaFitte's orders, so he hanged the culprit.

Realistically, nobody could control such a lawless crowd and soon, the United States again fell victim. This time, the United States captured and hung two of the perpetrators. Public sentiment declared the pirate's nest had to be cleaned out, but The United States government was slow to act. Nature was not so lenient. In 1820, a violent storm struck the unprotected island. Many vessels were sunk and much damage was done. Maison Rouge collapsed on the mixed crew and women who had gathered there for safety. Food supplies were ruined. As a relief measure, LaFitte seized all negroes on the island and shipped them off to the New Orleans slave markets.

This brought angry protests from some of the men who lived with the women.

The Karankawas, a tribe of Indian cannibals had long lived in the area. Pirates, lawless as usual, stole one of their squaws. In retaliation, the Karankawas ambushed, killed and ate four of the pirates. A general battle called the Battle of Three Trees followed. The pirates won the battle, but suffered further losses. When they received orders from the United States Government to depart, they left, but they left Campechi in flames. Only the wrecked Red House remained. No one really knows what became of them."

"You mean they simply vanished? The whole population?"

"Yes, the rest is legend. No other factual history remains."

"And that was Galveston? Wow! What a story."

"If that was the case there must be treasure..." Richard began.

"Of course," I exclaimed. "Buried all over the island. But—" I shook my head. "I can't imagine I would want to find it. Not that stuff, there's probably a curse or something on it."

"I don't know," said LeJuene. "Legend has it there are buried treasures hidden here, from all over the world."

"Well, you can have 'em," I said, making a face. "It gives me the creeps just to think about the pirates and their spoils."

"What happened to Galveston, next?" asked Etta, who had stood by, sullen in facial expression and in her posture.

"Nothing unusual happened for a while. In 1834, I believe, Michel B. Menard and nine English associates formed a company and secured title to four thousand, six hundred acres, and founded the present city of Galveston. During the Mexican war, it became a naval base."

"Yes, and it became Capital of Texas before the battle of San Jacinto," Richard put in.

"That's true. By the time of the Civil War, it had a population of ten thousand. Commander William B. Renshaw of the Union forces took over. The Confederates assembled a 'cotton-clad' armada—boats piled high with cotton bales which turned the cannon balls and they retook the city. 'Juneteenth' originated here by the way. General Gordon Granger set the slaves free on June 19, 1865."

"Do you know I have been raised among Negroes, and never even heard of 'Juneteenth' until I came down here?"

"Things go along at such a quiet and peaceful way in Mississippi, according to mother, that those things are given little thought," commented Etta sarcastically.

"Well, I think Galveston is a lovely city now. It is hard to think it had such a colorful history."

Henry, who had listened with great interest, contributed, "After Congress spent $6,800,000 on this harbor about eleven years ago, it really grew. The jetties are built of huge granite blocks. They extend five to seven miles out into the bay to shield the harbor from storms and break up pounding waves."

"Wasn't last year's population 38,000?" Richard wanted to know.

"About that, and growing steadily," replied LeJuene. "But I say, enough history. How about some fishing?"

"Yes!" we chorused and preparations were immediately under way.

Chapter 15 – Fishing

The White Swan contained every convenience for deep-sea fishing, the Sport of Kings, and I found it exciting sport indeed. Henrietta engaged a huge tarpon and screamed for our host. LeJuene took his place behind the girl, who was belted tightly into her mounted, rotating chair. Reaching around her with both arms and placing his hands, so slender, yet obviously strong, over hers, the battle began. Back and forth, reeling, slacking, reeling, slacking, as the monster fought and finally tired. At first I watched the fish as it leaped and shook, submerged and leaped again, seeking to dislodge the hook. Then I became aware of an obvious chemistry in the pair playing the fish that seemed completely unrelated to the battle. I felt embarrassed and moved a few steps away. *Etta is a wild young thing and perhaps this trip was not a good idea after all, especially as our chaperone, Viney, is seasick and had to go to bed. It is foolish for a child like Etta to throw herself at a man like LeJuene. He is probably embarrassed at her lack of reserve. There's a difference between impulsiveness and having no poise, or restraint.* At last the long battle with the great fish was over.

It floated exhausted alongside the boat, a sleek monster of the deep made captive by a silken line.

Stretching their backs and arms, the two fishermen stood. "Isn't it a beauty!" Henrietta exclaimed. "I could have never landed him except for your help, Andre," she added with an adoring look into his eyes.

"A case where two pairs of hands were definitely better than one, my dear." LeJuene laughed, and turned to his assembled guests,

"I think that calls for a drink. Thibodeaux, bring the liquors. We shall drink out here."

How am I going to get out of this? Fortunately the steward came first to Suellen and Ruth.

"No thanks," Suellen waved the drinks away, "I cut my teeth on rum and found that grape juice agrees with me better."

"I like my punch without the 'punch' too, if you know what I mean." Ruth also waved the steward away.

"Well, Tib, you'd better bring a round of lemonade for the ladies. All who prefer this punch help yourselves."

"Do you mean just ladies?" Tom Lowe staggered down the deck. "I can't walk straight on this boat anyway. When I pick my feet up the deck comes with me, and when I put them down, it isn't there. Give me the hills of Austin or even a bucking bronc, but don't ask me to complicate this trip with anything stronger than water."

LeJuene's face darkened, but he said good naturedly, "This sea is like velvet. I'd like to see you in a blow. Maybe you just don't like the 'nectar of the gods.'"

"You're right. I don't. May I have lemonade, please?" Tom reached for a glass.

"Well, I like mine with the punch included," Henrietta chose a drink from the tray.

"So do I," said several others as the steward passed the tray around.

"Good." Our host lifted his glass, "A toast then, to the luckiest fisherman of the day, and to us all, 'long life and good fishing.'" Everyone lifted their glasses to Henrietta, but she only had eyes for LeJuene.

The afternoon passed swiftly, with some bowling, shuttleboards, card games and laughter against a setting of cloudless sky, the gentle motion of the sea, and pleasant music from a phonograph in the lounge. In chairs along the afterdeck, we sat quietly and enjoyed the "magic moment" of twilight. I remembered and treasured again, the poignancy of my first experience of the "magic moment" on the curving balcony of The Fort.

Out of the quiet, Ruth spoke, "There is something about a twilight that casts a spell upon us all. See how peaceful we are after all that noisy chatter. What is it?"

"Maybe it has something to do with day's end. It brings us face to face with endings. That time we all try to put away from us when we ourselves must come to an ending," James reflected.

"Perhaps that is why it makes me think of home. If I try, I can imagine day's end on the plantation. I can almost hear the cowbells tinkling, nearer and nearer, until you hear the cows lowing. I can imagine the clank of trace chains and the sound of wagon wheels whistling through the sand, the hands coming in from the fields, the slap of a rein on a horse's flank. Then father will come home and before long, we will all be at supper, safe and snug, the lamps lighted against the dusk. Evening doesn't seem like parting to me. It seems like reunion."

"Hmm, perhaps that is what death is, not parting, but reunion," the boy from Dallas murmured.

Uncomfortable with the turn the conversation was taking, LeJuene suggested, "Maybe that's why I don't like twilight—its implications are too sobering. I don't like death—too final. I like life, and all I can crowd into it of pleasure and enjoyment. I don't know much about that Grand Tomorrow, someone else can look after that when I am gone. I am going to take what I can and enjoy it."

Surprised at such a negative comment, I responded, "Well, I think twilight is a lovely part of the day. Sometimes it is parting for friends, but most people return to family and the loved circle of home folks—a time of gathering, with the world shut out and the loved ones closed in together,"

"I guess that is why we miss them most at twilight," Suellen murmured softly. "My favorite brother was killed in a freak rodeo accident. I really miss him.'"

"It's the happiest hour when shared, and the loneliest time of the day when one is alone," suggested Hugh. Henry laid his hand on mine.

"I hear this hillbilly humming. Her worst vice is music. It gets all stirred up inside her and if not encouraged to escape, it can explode unexpectedly. Shall we let her explode or shall we ask her to sing?"

"Sing for us, by all means." LeJuene seconded, relieved to end the philosophical turn of the conversation.

"Do sing for us, Nancy. What was that you were humming? It has a lovely melody."

"Well, It just seems to fit. It's called 'The End of a Perfect Day.'"

While the long boat drifted on the quiet sea, and each communed with his or her own thoughts, I sang in a voice vibrant with feeling,

"When you come to the end of a perfect day;
And you sit alone with your thoughts.
When the chimes ring out with a carol gay,
For the joys that the day has brought.
Do you think what the end of a perfect day
Can mean to a tired heart?
As the sun goes down with a flaming ray,
And the dear friends have to part.

Well this is the end of a perfect day,
Near the end of a journey, too,
But it brings a thought that is big and strong
With wish that is kind and true.
For memory has painted this perfect day
With colors that never fade,
And you find at the end of a perfect day,
The heart of a friend you've made."

As I sang, LeJuene joined with his vibrant baritone. The daylight dimmed out and the lovely, brilliant coral color of sea and air lived its fleeting moment. Darkness covered the sky with a sable curtain, against which the stars became visible as if by magic. A "Magic Moment." The spell was upon us all. I felt Henry lean close as the darkness came. I pressed his hand.

After a peaceful moment, with only the shush of waves whispering against the boat, our host broke the silence.

"Lovely. I shall remember this moment and the song. But now, you will all wish to dress for dinner and dancing. I believe each of you knows the way to your quarters." A sigh ran through the group like people in a dream as we departed.

Chapter 16 – Charmed

The group shared a long, lovely evening with pleasant music, laughter, conversation, and dancing on the gently rocking Swan. LeJuene devoted himself to me in a most flattering way. His charm and my reaction to it puzzles me. I know I love Tom, and thrill at the memory of his kiss. But this man is a new experience. Something about him draws me—a mysterious magnetism that challenges and somehow almost frightens me. It is as if I am wandering on the edge of an unknown forest, determined to find out what is in its shadowed depths. I laughed aloud.

"What thoughts I am thinking!"

"Shall we take a turn around the deck? It is cooler outside and the moon is worth investigating."

"I would like that." Outside, LeJuene took my arm to steady me against the gentle rolling of the boat. At his touch, I felt again my contradictory emotions. His hand seemed to burn my arm, and somehow I felt uneasy at his touch. It was confusing, but as he spoke in his low, charming voice of places he had been, and of his home on the moss-draped bayou, I forgot my slight uneasiness and felt myself coming under his spell. It was as if I left the ship to explore with him the shaded bayou he described, where hyacinth and water lilies covered the streams. I laughed again.

"What is it that amuses you?" he asked. "Twice you have laughed at your own thoughts. Will you not share them with me?"

"Oh, I was just thinking about you. You appeal to my romantic nature. I see you with swashbuckling swords, romance, and mystery. Yet, I am not sure I like you. You draw me, but my mind draws me back. I am laughing at myself. Forgive me, please. I laughed at the absurd imagery of my own imagination. It seemed like I was standing at the edge of the forest, wishing I knew what was hidden in its dense shade, yet afraid to explore. LeJuene was silent for a time. Then he reached and took a rose tucked into my belt. He began to pluck its petals.

"Do not be afraid, little Nancy. I, too, recognize that we are different. You have been so sheltered in your Mississippi home. There is so much of life that you do not know. What a pleasure it would be to teach you. Perhaps we shall explore it together, you and I. I have a feeling I shall influence your life. But right now, I want to hear you sing. Let's go aloft to the wheelhouse where we shall be alone, but for the night and the sea." Together, we climbed the short stair. Removing his coat, LeJuene seated me on it, with my back to the housing. He took own seat, half reclining at my feet.

"Sing to me a song of the night, Nancy. No, sing me a song of love."

"Why not both?" I laughed self-consciously.

"Both? Splendid."

So in my best rich voice, I sang.

"Day must pass and night will follow after,
Bringing darkness with its somber hue.
All the lanes are filled with strolling lovers,
Whispering the words I say to you.
Just a little love, a little kiss,
I would give you all the world for this.

On the last line, I trilled up the octave with my best light trill. LeJuene joined with his full deep voice in perfect harmony. As the notes died away, he turned with a quick roll and took me in his arms.

"Do you know how I feel about you, Little Nancy? You are as lovely as the night, as fragile as our Louisiana water flowers. I would indeed give all the world for this." Bending swiftly, he sought my lips. Just as swiftly, thinking of Tom, I turned my cheek.

"No? You rejected my kiss. But ah, Little Nancy, your heart beats madly, like a fluttering bird. You do not give me the answer I want, but you shall. I notice you do not drink this evening, but one day you will." Touching her curls, he told her, "I shall teach you. One day you will drink champagne with me. One day you will give me your lips, and you will be more beautiful than ever—like the apple tree when she is in full bloom. You shall see, sweet Nancy, that you and I shall reach the heights together. You gave me your cheek tonight, but we shall see...."

I could feel my heart pounding. It seemed it would smother me. I forced myself to stand.

"What a poet! No wonder I imagined you in velvet and a powdered wig. Your other guests must be wondering where their host is. Shall we return to the party?"

Long after the Swan had docked and the party dispersed, after I was at home in bed, the pounding of my senses continued. In my mind, I still hovered around the edge of that imagined forest, peering excitedly into its beckoning mystery. Viney watched me with her shrewd eyes. Just before turning out the light, she covered my smooth white hand with her wrinkled black one.

"Miss Nancy, Baby, don't you let dat Frenchman turn yo haid. He ain't no ways like yo people. His life is different, his whole way uv looking at life ain't one bit like yorn! An' Viney sho don't want to see you get hurt!"

"Oh, Viney, he wouldn't hurt me. He is different, but I like him. He is suave, more worldly, so charming. I don't see why the way *we* look at things has to be the only way. I never have been satisfied. Maybe 'dat Frenchman' is just what I've been looking for."

"Oh Lawd, I wish yo mamma was here! How 'm I gonna make you understan'? It's like dis Miss Nancy. Now Mr. Tom, fer instance. To him, you be de comin' true of dreams. His whole life, to de longest day you live, he'd treasure you. Make you know he loved you. Spen' his life shelterin' you from anything dis ole world could do to disappoint you. He wouldn't wan nothin outside uv lovin' you. His whole world would be jis you, and a makin' his way fer yo' sake. Bein' a man for yo' sake, buildin' a home for yo' sake. He'd love you completely, wid all de world outside. You know how it is wid yo' Momma. Yo' Pappa, he's crazy 'bout her. I ain't never heard them say nothin' mean to each other in all they lives. Yo Pappa always shows he loves her an' treats her like he done when they was sweethearts—like you an Mr. Tom. He's proud of her an' not 'shamed to show it. Now wid dat "Playboy" it's different.

Mr. Tom, he won't need no mo' romance cause he fine all de romance he need in you. But dat man—long as he live he goin'a chase de ladies. You jis anudder sompin' what he wants. You marry him, he'll spen' his money on you, and when it humor him he'll flatter you, but you aint gonna no way interfere wid de way he lives. You jus be awaitin', and when he wants to see you, he'll come around. Dat aint no life fer you, Miss Nancy. You done been raised where mens looks on ladies as somthin' to love an' look after, to live wid, an be true to. Dey puts you fust and somethin' makin' you happy is what dey wants. I aint gonna no way, let you be no background plaything fur no Frenchman." I got out of bed, hugged my beloved mammy and friend and teased, "Viney, you're a regular preacher. I'm *not* going to marry the man, but I do like him, and I'm glad I met him. We're going to have some fun, that's all. Now scat, and get some sleep."

"Well... goodnight, Sweet Girl. But don't you go getting' no ideas in yo haid 'bout dat man. I done promise yo poppa I'd look after you, an' I aims to do it, too."

Chapter 17 – The Real Dream

"Good morning, sweet chile. What you want'a wear this mornin'?" Thursday had dawned clear, but I could hear the ever-present wind. I hummed the melody of wind and waves woven into "The Majesty of the Sea." This day was to be another round of gaiety. "Let's see, we are going to swim early, before it gets too hot. Just get out something simple, so we can go down to breakfast. Oh, my goodness, Viney. I'm having so much fun. I'm just loving Galveston, the ocean, the flowers, the people—I may never be ready to go home to Mississippi."

At the look of shock on my beloved mammy's face, I giggled and exclaimed, "Gotcha that time didn't I? Just teasing, but I *am* having a wonderful time, and I can hardly wait for tonight. I'll wear Great Aunt Nancy's gown, jewels, and carry her ivory fan. You can fix my hair just like hers. I will be like the picture in the drawing room at home, come to life. The group from the cruise is planning dinner at the club, before the ball begins. James Dies, the young man from Dallas, is going to call for me. Henry and Henrietta and their dates, are included for the dinner, even though they are younger."

"Nancy, don't you never skeer me like dat agin," said the

old woman, fanning her face. "Now hustle, Chatter Box, or we gonna be late for breakfast." She helped me dress quickly, and we hurried downstairs. The day passed leisurely, with swimming, tennis, and shopping.

At lunch, I turned to the Captain, "It is so different, swimming in the ocean from swimming at home. Our swimming hole, Roger's Branch, was created by a spring fed creek. Where the water drops over a rock outcrop, it made a large hole, fifty feet or more in diameter. We're not allowed 'mixed swimming,' so the boys have their turn, and when they are gone, we girls have our turn. I've heard the boys don't even wear swim suits."

He almost choked on his food, as he burst out laughing. "I expect that is right. When I was a boy, we called that skinny dipping."

I blushed but continued, "With trees all around, the creek is always shady, so the water is very cold and as clear as glass. Sometimes we kids wade the sandy bottom from the pool, all the way down the creek to the Chickasawhay River. We find those same odd shells you call sand dollars in our creek bed."

Tears glistened in Aunt Grace's eyes as she reminisced. "You certainly bring back happy memories of my childhood. I also waded in Roger's Branch, but we girls were not allowed to swim. Somewhere, I still have a little sand dollar necklace my Poppa had made for me from a shell I picked up in that creek. Well, we'd all better have a quiet rest, before our big evening."

While all was quiet, I wrote long letters to Tom, and to my parents, describing the activities of the week.

Finally, it was time to don the costumes and get ready for the ball. With trembling fingers Viney fussed about, helping me into the dainty garments and wide hoopskirt. She applied powder and dressed my hair. "Be still, chile, I sho don't wanna burn you wid dis hot curlin' iron." Then she fastened the ornate antique sapphire necklace around my neck and attached the matching earrings. Though she didn't say anything, I knew Viney brooded with misgiving because LeJuene was to be at the party. I didn't say anything either, because there was no use arguing with my old mammy who would never approve of LeJuene. *How absurd. Andre is a man of culture and refinement, wealth, and even noble ancestry. He is a polished and charming man. Viney's just being oldfashioned and silly.*

Finished, curled and powdered, I looked into the mirror with my blue-grey eyes shining. *This is my big dream, finally come to life. And somehow, LeJuene is part of the wonder of it.* Gathering up my mask, fan and silk handkerchief, I started down the blue carpeted stairs. Hearing my steps, the folks waiting in the parlor looked up. Startled by their stares, I paused at the turn of the stairway, not realizing the picture I made in my hoop-skirted rose taffeta gown with its tiny brocade flowers, and bouffant skirt. Fine lace edged the tight bodice and lay back from my smooth white shoulders. The wide off-the-shoulder neckline showed Great Aunt Nancy's gorgeous sapphire necklace perfectly. And truth to tell, showed more of me than I was accustomed to showing. On my ear lobes, wrist, and finger, and in the upright comb atop my curls, the same blue jewels glistened. One large pink rose adorned my waistline and a smaller one at the side of my hair graced my face. My eyes must have reflected my excitement. A male voice from downstairs broke my trance, exclaiming,

"Nancy, you lovely lady, you make a picture to take one's breath away!" I realized I appeared to be posing on the curving mahogany stairway, and my knees almost gave way as I realized how conspicuous I was just standing there. I blushed, smiled and moved as gracefully as I could on down the stairs. The gentlemen all watched, but Henry was first with his hand outstretched to assist me.

"Nancy, you are amazing. I have never seen anyone so beautiful." The rest of the family complimented me and James proudly tucked my hand into his arm.

"Am I escorting this gorgeous lady tonight? I'll be so conceited Dallas will not be able to contain me. I feel like the prince in the Cinderella story. Miss Norsworthy, I hope you are not wearing glass slippers." I poked out a toe.

"Not glass, Mr. Dies. Satin. And you are safe. I promise, if our carriage does not turn into a pumpkin, I will not turn into a scullery maid until midnight." Chuckles rippled through the crowd, putting every one at ease.

Dies was costumed as a dressed up Texas cowboy, with beautifully tooled, hand made boots, matching belt and gauntlets, silk shirt that matched his eyes, and a kerchief around his neck. I complemented, "James, your boots and gauntlets are works of art. Do you suppose I could commission the craftsman to make a set for me before I go back to Mississippi?"

"I will be glad to put you in touch with Jose. He makes boots for three generations of my family. The last pair he made for my mother are her favorites." James self-consciously turned his elegant, white Stetson hat in his hands.

The twins dressed as the famous French puppets, Perriot and Perriette, while Captain and Mrs. Hand were elaborately groomed as George and Martha Washington. To my surprise, just before we left for the party, a clown with a painted face, an orange wig, and dressed in huge shoes, white gloves, a ballooning, striped suit, and a tall Lincolnesque black top hat stepped silently through the parlor door. Aunt Grace and the

Captain laughed. The clown bowed, made an exaggerated wink at me, and spoke in a familiar voice.

"I ain't never been to a costume party afore, and Miz Hand, she order me dis costume and wig an things. She paint my face an fix me up to go. She say, "Viney, you ken be the Cinderella this time. Ifen I be quiet an' they bring me home afore time to take off they masks, who'll know the difference?" Everyone laughed and promised to diligently guard Viney's secret.

* * * * *

The Club Verien had never looked lovelier than when festively adorned for this ball. The fragrance of fresh roses mingled with the scent of multitudes of glowing candles. The elegance of the tables, set with fine crystal and exquisite china reminded me of the Governor's ball in Jackson. For just a moment, I felt guilty that Tom was missing all of this, and no doubt, missing me.

Some of the party were already seated, and the gentlemen rose to meet our group. LeJuene wore romantic Spanish Cavalier attire, and by his side sat a dark-eyed Carmen, the same Charlotte DeArmen who had been his companion at that first luncheon. I looked at this girl and saw beauty, dignity, breeding, and perfect manners. But a hard shell seemed to bind her. *I'm afraid I could never be as sophisticated as she is.* My dinner placement, between LeJuene and James, with Henry across the table, was perfect. The elegant, candlelit table, the gourmet meal, and the orchestra imported from New Orleans, were all superb. The beautiful costumes, quivering violins, and growing awareness of my own loveliness thrilled me. These things fit perfectly into my old romantic dream. Add the strangely magnetic presence of LeJuene and I was virtually intoxicated with excitement.

I danced with LeJuene, and as we were returning to our table, the orchestra suddenly began to play to my favorite music, "The Bell Song." At my elbow. Andre whispered, "Sing," and joy spilled from me as I burst into singing. Bright as bird's song, clear as sunlight on water, my voice filled the room. Behind me, LeJuene joined with harmony in his full, deep voice. Staying ever in the background, touching my hands lightly, he guided my serenade from one table to another. Skillfully, LeJuene maneuvered so the song concluded before the open French doors. Bowing, he drew me quickly out onto the moonlit balcony, as applause swept the room. "Little Nancy, you are incredible. You, that gown, and your amazing voice. These jewels," he touched a finger to the necklace, "are not half so lovely as you. This time you shall not give me the cheek, little Nancy. You and I have emotions the world does not share. Is it not so?" The handsome turned lips above his white teeth were slowly drawing nearer. I trembled inwardly. This man threw my senses into a tumult. I seemed incapable of turning away.

"Oh, excuse me. I thought I had left my scarf out here." Henrietta's red face appeared in the doorway. The interruption, and the look on Etta's face, brought me back to the present and reality. I suppose Etta resented me "making a spectacle" of myself, as Viney would say. The younger girl and her partner danced away, but the spell was broken. I was glad—yet strangely regretful, too.

"We must get back to the party." I turned to the open door.

"Not that way. Over here," and smoothly LeJeune steered me around the balcony to enter by another door. He had regained his regal bearing, and I could hardly believe the moment on the balcony had even occurred. The poise with which he carried it off chilled me slightly and I chilled further when I saw the cold unreadable glance I received from his lady friend, Charlotte. Thoroughly repressed, I picked up my antique Spanishlace mantilla and threw it around my shoulders. I paused by Aunt Grace to whisper, "I've done it again. What must you think of me?" She patted my hand.

"Well, we love your singing Nancy, but I am glad your parents aren't here. I am afraid they would hardly approve. So public, you know."

"I do know, and I am so sorry." I hurriedly returned to my seat, and for the rest of the meal I devoted myself to my escort, James. I hardly dared to look at LeJuene.

Toward the close of the meal, a man in medieval costume appeared and bowed to Captain Hand. "Pardon this intrusion, Sir, but I heard the young lady sing. Music is my business and hers is no ordinary voice. She should have an audition at the Metropolitan. Here is my card, and whenever you like, we can arrange it." I blushed, "But I could never be that good."

"You let me be the judge of that, young lady. I know a great gift when I encounter one."

LeJuene broke in, "I'll tell you what we will do. There is reported to be a storm in the Gulf south of Louisiana. It will probably pass this way, but when it clears we can take the White Swan and sail around the coast to New York. I have a large apartment there. After your audition, Nancy, I can give you a tour of the Big Apple. You will love Vaudeville."

Pulling my shawl more tightly around my shoulders, I quickly replied, "I could not accept such extended hospitality. Besides, I have no desire for a public career."

"Nonsense, just think of it! That voice will have the world at your feet."

I laughed nervously, remembering what my poppa had said

to Mr. Lofton last summer, "But I don't want the world at my feet. I just want to sing when I'm happy, and to make others happy."

"Yes. That is just it! Think of the thousands who would thrill to your joyousness. Isn't that what music is for?"

"Never the less, I'm sure I should not be interested."

To my surprise, I heard Captain Hand say, "I don't know, Nancy. As I said once before, a voice like that belongs to the world." *Maybe I should consider it. It all seems impossible and far away, but why not? A whole new world might be opening before me. Maybe my voice is important.* The next part of the evening passed in a blur. When I looked up again, Henry was dancing merrily with the clown!

My world seemed to be turning topsy-turvey. Rather late I slipped away and wandered out to the balcony alone, turning this new idea over in my mind. *A quiet, good life with Tom's love and devotion, or the glittering fulfillment of a career. I know Tom would never approve a public career for me, but LeJeune?*

Suddenly below me in the darkness I heard LeJuene's throaty, teasing chuckle. Then I heard Etta's agitated voice, "Oh Andre. This whole evening has been torment. It isn't enough to have her here, so cool and sure of herself, but now you have to go chasing after Nancy. I can't sing, it's true, and I haven't all those airs but I can give you something she can't and I will show you." There was a momentary silence. Astonished, I hesitated. *Is the poor child mad? How awful for Mr. LeJuene to have her throw herself at him this way."*

But, from the darkness came the mesmerizing voice. "Um-um! That was quite a kiss! But you would never enter into a really adult relation. You're only playing at love. You don't know what you are driving at!"

"Ohhh don't I? Andre. you dunce, I worship you. It drives me crazy to look at Charlotte and know what she is to you."

"So, …you arrived at that understanding?"

"Of course. And now Nancy—She is such an innocent saint. She probably thinks you want to marry her. And she will fall for it thinking that. Oh, I could just kill her! I don't want you to kiss anybody but me. I'd do anything—*anything*, to have you all for myself."

"My goodness, the little red head really means it!

"Of course I mean it, Andre. I am crazy for you. That baby Sam. Always wanting me to marry him. After you, it's like kissing a rag doll. Oh Andre, what can I do to prove it to you."

"But, Little Etta, you are not my kind. We would have a terrible time. You wouldn't know your place. Now, Charlotte…."

"I can be anything to you that she can be. I'll show you. I'll come to your rooms tomorrow night."

"Hmmm. That could be interesting! If you come… "

"I'm coming. You'll see."

"No, you wouldn't really, You are just talking."

"I will, too. I'll show you what I can do!"

"Well, I will be out of town tomorrow night. If you came, I wouldn't be there."

"Sunday then, I'll be there when you come home."

"Interesting, of course—if you come." Laughing, he ran up the steps to the balcony and passed me where I had stepped back in darkness.

I flushed bitterly with resentment. So that was what lay beyond the edge of the forest. And I, level headed Nancy, had been tempted to enter that unknown forest. Indignantly I turned and re-entered the ballroom. To my amazement, LeJuene was waltzing with Aunt Grace, being very gay and charming as usual. I sank limply into my chair. Surely Etta would think...realize her youth and the disaster of such conduct. She would get over it. Of course that was it. Later, when LeJuene claimed me for a dance, I was cordial, giving no hint of what I had heard. I promised to think it over when he again mentioned the New York trip, but assured him if I went, it would be on one of Mr. Hand's ships, and I would stay at a hotel while I was there.

"But I shall go too, Nancy. You shall not escape sharing the big city with me. It will be my pleasure to show you the city. I know it well, and you shall enjoy it with me."

The old spell was working. In spite of everything, the thrilling prospect became brighter as I thought of sharing the Big City with LeJuene.

"We will talk about it later when I have decided if I shall go."

Going home, my mind swam with the surprises of the evening, but to be fair to my cowboy escort, I kept up a cheerful conversation with him. James had been a perfect gentleman all evening, but my mind was in such turmoil, I was glad when I could thank him for a delightful evening and say, "Goodnight."

Henrietta, the poor child! Would Etta actually go to LeJuene's rooms? Does he not realize Etta's reckless temperament? What if she does go? Oh mercy, I must do something to prevent it. Maybe talk to Aunt Grace? I blanched at the thought of telling my mother's sweet friend what her daughter planned to do. Henry then? It would be useless to talk to Henry. What can I do? Talk to LeJuene? Huh, am I just deceiving myself? How do I know he doesn't intend to take advantage of her immaturity? But—he is so nice—isn't he? Is Charlotte really what Etta said?" My head was in a whirl. It seemed unthinkable to stand by and do nothing to prevent my young friend from taking this degrading action. A sudden realization struck me. *What right do I have to question the child's behavior? I am fascinated with LeJuene myself. I stood in the moonlight pondering my dilemma. Should I trust LeJuene or doubt his integrity? Was Viney's judgment right… again?*

"Heavenly Father," *I prayed silently,* "what should I do? Please give me wisdom and courage."*(James 1:5 NIV)*

* * * * *

As I started up the stairs to my room, a hand reached out and detained me. "Nancy, please come out here on the balcony. I need to talk to you." *Oh, Henry knows. Perhaps there is a way to manage this after all!* But on the balcony, Henry stood silent. He picked up one of my hands and played with my fingers.

"Nancy, since you came here, I have been trying to show you a good time. You probably think I am just a kid, but I am not. I really work at Father's office, serious, responsible work. He will make me a partner some day. I'm supposed to go to college, but a formal education is not necessary. Experience is all I need to carry on the business. I know I'm a bit younger than you, but a few years one way or the other don't really matter."

"What are you saying, Henry? Do you want advice about college?"

"No, Nancy. What I am trying to say is, I want you to marry me. Nancy, you are in every way the loveliest person I have ever met. I've watched you ever since you have been here and I love you with all my heart. You are so fine, so sweet and lovely. Nancy, I could pull myself out of this 'coastal madness' we live in here if you would help me. Do I stand a chance? Oh, Nancy, I love you so much." Fiercely, he pressed my hand to his lips. To my horror, I felt his tears on my hand.

"Henry." I put a hand on his shoulder, "my dear friend, I

never dreamed of anything like this. You have been like the brother I never had. I am afraid I could never love you in that way. Can't we just be friends, Henry?" My heart clenched as I saw his face go white, and his chin tremble.

"I'm so sorry!" I patted his arm.

"I guess we can just be friends, Nancy, but I can never forget how much I love you. Are you sure I don't stand a chance?"

"Quite sure, Henry, and I am terribly sorry. I had no idea—I wouldn't hurt you for anything in the world."

"Very well, I wont make a nuisance of myself. But, I shall never forget you, and no one else can ever love you more completely than I do."

"Henry, I have no words to tell you how I feel. This takes me completely by surprise. I can only hope you can forgive me quickly. And thank you, dear, for loving me." Standing on tiptoes, I kissed him gently on the forehead.

"Goodnight, Nancy, but I won't forget. Loving you may not mean the kind of happiness I hoped for, but I'll let it help me to be a man–the kind of gentleman, that you are a lady. So don't worry about me, I'll be okay." Though clearly hurt, he waved me toward the staircase with tears in his eyes and a shaky smile on his lips. Gratefully, I gathered up my skirts and ran.

I stopped before entering my room and again prayed, "Heavenly Father, You promise wisdom to those who ask. Please—I need it now." My head is spinning—*Henry, Henrietta, LeJuene, Charlotte, audition, New York, Tom, career, Momma, Poppa, Viney, a clown....*the rising winds lashing the ocean are no more turbulent than my churning emotions. *What should I do?*

Whew—maybe tomorrow I will calm down and think clearly.

Chapter 18 – Anticipation

September 7, 1900

Saturday dawned gloomy. A deeper booming sounded from the ocean. White caps scudded along the waves. A strong wind blew incessantly. About ten o'clock, the Captain called from his office.

"There are storm warnings out. The hurricane is moving this way and will probably strike today, but there is nothing to worry about. You know we often have storms, and even unusually high water never does much damage."

Aunt Grace reassured me, "This round house was built to stand against storms. It is high enough on its rock foundation and stout enough to stand against any storm." Hourly, the storm grew stronger. It blew in great gusts like some wicked giant breathing. The sea became more agitated, the rollers higher. Reassured by my hostess, I felt a keen exhilaration from the spectacle. It was exciting to safely observe such turmoil of nature.

After lunch, Henry said, "Get your boots and a slicker on, Nancy. We are going down to the docks. The wind is blowing from that direction and Dad says the waves are something to see!" As we stood on the dock, I saw a sight I would never forget. In wild agitation, small boats strained at their anchors. Some had broken loose and were tossed about on the waves. A few had broken loose, and with each surge seemed to sink a little deeper out of sight. Born on the wild wind, the waves were like giant piled up wrinkles sweeping endlessly in to the shore. They hit the concrete bulkhead with shattering force, shooting straight up, high into the air before falling back to retreat and then charge again. It was a magnificent spectacle that I could have watched for hours.

I remembered the conversation with the captain of the White Swan. "Galveston would be hit first by a north wind. It would then blow counter-clockwise in a circle." I shivered in spite of myself. Before dinner that night, I asked Captain Hand about the progress of the storm. "Well, the weather bureau says it will pass to the south of us. The center is well out in the gulf. We will only get the northern edge of it. Strange thing, this storm is a deviation from the norm. They usually pass north over the Atlantic seaboard. This one came north over Cuba after traveling west from the Leeward Islands. It seems bent on carving out its own path. But its course is south of us, so I guess Galveston has nothing to fear."

"I giggled. In that case, I'm glad I didn't miss it. It is the most exciting performance of nature I have ever seen. The power of those waves as they rush against the pier, leaping high into the air, then falling back, and surging again, thrills me. It is amazing how puny man is able to hold such force in check."

"Yes, Galveston is built to withstand the elements, and lying as it does, in the curve of the coastline, it is probably safe from much storm destruction. The weather bureau predicted it would strike tonight, but the wind seems to be dying down, so apparently, it passed south of us in the open gulf. That would account for these waves we are having. The northwest wind we have been feeling is evidently the crown of the hurricane circle which has now passed beyond us."

"Whew, that is a relief, but I can't begin to tell you how the excitement and activity of the elements thrills me." I laughed again, exhilarated by this brand new experience.

Aunt Grace, the former landlocked Mississippian, sought to reassure me.

"I well remember my first experiences with coastal storms. What do you say we watch it for a while from the observatory?"

"Let's do! What a perfect observation spot you built, Captain Hand."

Together, we climbed to the Crow's Nest where the wind howled with an unearthly voice. Out before us stretched scudding white-capped waves, in terrible agitation under a somber sky. As we watched, a startling thing occurred. A momentary gap appeared in the cloud curtain and strange, greenish sunlight poured through, bathing land and sea in unearthly light. Through the rift, an awesome apparition appeared—a swollen blood red disk of sun against the sickly green sky. I had never seen anything like it.

"Wow! It looks as big as a wash tub," I cried, but the horizon was already chewing at the edge of the sun and with one last peep of fiery edge, it was gone. The clouds closed again and the darkness was insistent. To the East, the Bolivar lighthouse winked its faithful eye. Somewhere, a bell buoy clamored. "It must have been on just such a night as this "Asleep In the Deep" was written, and I began to sing,

"Loudly the bell in the old tower rings.
Bidding us list' to the warning it brings.
Sailor take care. Sailor take care.
Danger is near thee, beware, be...ware!
Many brave hearts are asleep in the deep
So beware! Beware!"

I have a wide vocal range, so though I usually sing high and lightly, I surprised everyone with the vibrant deep-pitched warning. When I finished, all was silent for a moment.

"Beautifully done, my dear, but the warning comes a little late," the Captain assured us. See, the wind is gradually dying. At this rate, by midnight, all will be calm."

"Yes, and the servants probably think we are waiting for midnight to come to dinner." Aunt Grace led the way down to the dining room.

Ever the gentleman, Captain Hand waited for the others to precede him, and the young folks walked together, holding hands. I had enjoyed the wild wind, but it was a relief to have it dying down. So much excitement can be exhausting.

"Well, the Chamber of Commerce will be glad it is over," remarked Henry. Now the Sunday Excursion can come as usual. It brings a fat profit for Galveston merchants.

"Yes and for liquor dealers, gamblers, and others, I would rather not mention. I don't like these excursions. They turn the city into a carnival."

"And on the Lord's Day, too," Aunt Grace echoed her husbands sentiments, "I hope I never get used to this habit of treating the Sabbath like a carnival."

"Oh, *you two*!" Etta piped up. "Always seeing the gloomy side. I think the excursions are fun—all the people coming and going. Everybody happy. I suppose you would rather everyone remained at home, sedately going to church and home again—how much fun is that?"

"Henrietta. I must insist you speak politely to your mother. If your thinking has been so influenced by your environment that it is impossible to agree, you still must speak respectfully to Mother."

"Sorry, Father." Etta said as we were seated for dinner.

Chapter 19 – Decision Time

The servants had all seen that brief, unearthly sun. They were muttering among themselves. The cook was singing mournfully as she rattled the pots and pans in the kitchen, a thing decidedly out of the ordinary in this smoothly running household. To my surprise, when it was time to retire, in spite of the fact that the weather was now perfectly calm, Viney walked in with her mattress on her shoulders and with determination, plunked it down at the foot of my bed. "Viney, what in the world are you doing?"

"I doan like the feel of things 'round here. Sompin' gonna happen, an when it does, I'm gonna be rat heah by you!"

"Why Viney! The wind is perfectly calm. Captain Hand says the storm is over. It passed us in the open gulf."

"I doan keer. I seed dat sun! My grammaw tole me 'bout seein' a sun like dat in Tahiti afore a bad storm. 'sides, I had a dream last night … " Viney stubbornly shook her head.

I laughed, but shivered. I was well acquainted with Viney's penchant for dreams. I hugged my Mammy. "Well, if it will make you happier to sleep on that hard floor, I guess I shouldn't complain."

"Taint no use. I'se gonna sleep right here jes the same. Yo Poppa tole me to take care of you and I'm gonna do it. I chuckled, but when I turned the light off and all was quiet, I found it hard to relax. The air was humid and clammy. I finally dozed and dreamed of a grinning, blood- red sun which Viney shook her fist at, and a fat man on a bell buoy was chanting in sepulchral tones, "Danger is near thee, beware, be . . . ware!"

I woke, surprised to find that the wind had risen, driving hard gusts of rain against the window. Throwing off the covers, I slept again. By morning the storm winds were clamoring. I remembered again what the captain of the Swan had said about hurricanes. Did the calm last night mean we are directly in the path of the storm?

Tension hung over the city. The renewed storm winds were more violent than ever. In the business district, rumors ran rampant. Some said the worst blow in history is on its way. Some people are leaving for the mainland. Some think the whole population should be evacuated! Absurd! According to the Captain, blows come and blows go, but they never amount to much ... a little high water, a few shingles blown away, perhaps a palm tree here or there maybe, but so what? It'll be over by night and is a good show while it lasts—a little excitement for the excursion crowd. They'll get a thrill out of seeing the city just after a blow.

The wind blew louder and stronger. Its spiteful breathing became an almost unbearable roar. The barometer glass was still falling, and waves grew higher. From time to time, Captain. Hand, at his office, called the house, checking conditions on the beach and reporting on the wharves, and the town. The battering waves were beginning to mount the bulkhead, sweeping in to flood the low areas of the city. Great waves from the gulf rolled higher, sweeping inland across the beach. Ever higher and wilder, the water lapped closer to the city. Warehouses began to go down on the wharf. Beach shacks caved in and rushed away on the surging waters.

An exodus began. Families trekked toward the central city and higher ground. Rich, poor, Negro, Indian, Mexican and white alike moved inland. In response to appeals from the council, all homes were opened to receive anyone who needed shelter. The confusion grew ever wilder. The elements of nature continuously became more violent. Shifting winds gave undeniable evidence that the city was caught in the vortex of the storm. The first winds, those we felt from the northwest, were now from southwest and south, as the spiral progressed with ever-increasing velocity. When he reported this news, Grace worried how anything could stand if the wind grew any stronger. Reason told her this must be the peak of the storm. This tumult was past excitement… It had become agonizing. The wildly screaming wind, the smashing of the waters, the whole world seemed to be in motion. *Should we take refuge in the city? I've never felt this anxious before.* She chided herself for worrying. *My wise husband will make that decision if we need to go.*

Henrietta prowled restlessly, stopping to peer calculatingly out a window. I, remembering Etta's reckless plan to sneak out and go to LeJuene this evening, was thankful for the rain and the storm. There was apparently no danger, and at least my young friend would be saved from her folly. Henry also suffered. However, I knew my rejection of his young love was a present pain from which he would recover.

Just before noon, the Captain phoned. "Grace, something terrible has happened. Stanley Spencer, Charles Killmer, and Richard Lord were sitting in Ritter's restaurant, drinking coffee and discussing the storm. They made light of the danger, and declared they would stay in the city, storm or no storm. At that very moment, a violent gust shook the building. The roof collapsed, crashing in on them. All three were killed instantly! Injury and confusion are spreading throughout the city. Things are bad here at the wharves. Some boats have broken anchor and smashed against the bulkhead. Buildings are being terribly shaken."

"Please come home, Honey. We need you to decide whether to risk staying here at The Fort. Do you think maybe we should come into town? The water is rising steadily and the house is shuddering from the impact of the wind." It seemed hours before he finally burst through the door, soaked to the skin. The force of the wind made closing the door extremely difficult. It took three of us pushing to get it closed.

"Oh dear! You are soaked." Grace threw a large towel about his shoulders. "What took so long?"

"I had a difficult time getting here. I had to ride the streetcar, come partway by boat, wade at last and then struggle up our driveway! Part of it is already submerged and the water is rising steadily. This promises to be the worst storm Galveston has ever seen. The barometer is already showing the lowest reading on record, and still falling. The water is past record high. I'm afraid there is going to be much suffering before this one is over."

"I am so glad you are home, dear. I felt uneasy about staying, yet hesitated about taking the responsibility for going into town. Should we stay or shall we go?"

"Well, there is no hurry. If the winds have not abated by late afternoon, I'll phone for a boat and we can spend the night in a hotel. Unless it becomes much worse, we are in no danger.

Our house has an elevation equal to the town and is securely built against the wind."

"I am so relieved to hear you say that. Of course I was aware of those facts, but it was just too big a decision for me to make alone."

"Well, let's have some lunch. I will keep in touch with the office by phone. We will keep watch, but I don't feel we have anything to worry about."

Chapter 20 – Apprehension

Conversation was nearly impossible. The pounding of the elements made hearing difficult and the atmosphere was so heavy, even a deep breath became a chore. Anxiety hovered in the air. The meal finished with little conversation and we retired to the drawing room while the Captain made a tour of inspection to observe the progress of the rising flood.

"Look at our driveway!" His exclamation brought us all to stand beside him. "This is worse than I thought. When I came home an hour ago, the waters were beginning to lick at the driveway, now look." It was an awesome sight. Most of the curving length of the drive, with its border of flowers and seashells had disappeared into the raging sea. Where it should have been, we saw only tossing, tumultuous waters.

Quietly, we all walked to the drawing room windows overlooking the ocean. All day, I had been conscious of the sound of the waters. Now we watched silently as the sea lashed angrily against the Fort's rock barricade and sprayed high into the air, falling back to rush again, just as it had at the wharf. There was no longer a beach, only ocean. The round promontory of The Fort with its tall dwelling, was like a lighthouse marooned on the angry sea. The garden had drowned in the rain. The sundial and benches disappeared in the flood.

"Do you think we should chance staying here?" Aunt Grace anxiously inquired. Her husband responded, "Let's give it a little longer. I can't help but think this must be the storm's peak. The line at the weather bureau is jammed, but I have a courier there who phones periodically to the office. They will keep in touch with me, so we will know where we stand. We are as safe from a flood here as we would be anywhere in town," he assured us.

"Quite true, dear. You built wisely. But still, our house is so alone and unprotected. It gets the full brunt of the wind."

"Don't worry, Grace, the Fort can withstand any wind and flood. However, just to be safe, I will call and check the progress of the wind. We can see the water for ourselves." The Captain laughed and went away to phone. When he returned, he said with guarded cheerfulness, "I had a time getting a line. Everybody in town must be phoning somebody else. This storm has everyone excited. Jennings says things are hopping out there at the harbor. Even some larger boats are breaking loose or straining at their anchors. Floodwaters are rising and he says the weather bureau insists the worst is yet to come. You know how that goes—they always try to scare you to death."

Aunt Grace smiled at me. "Everybody plus the weather bureau puts out reports every time we have a blow. They always warn us to prepare for the worst. Until you get used to it, it is very frightening. Then, first thing you know, the storm is over. The sun shines brightly, the waters calm, and the few timid souls who made an exodus inland, come back embarrassed and life goes on as usual. It must be threatening to you, but we have been through it all before."

"Oh, don't worry about me, Aunt Grace. I am perfectly willing to leave things in your capable hands." Quiet settled on the group in the drawing room. To me, it seemed we were all kind of in a state of suspended animation. Listening to the unspeakable fury of the storm, feeling the shudder of the unrelenting gale and just waiting…I stood by the drawing room window, eyes on the churning water. The waves crashed against the curved garden wall and swelled around the house. I could see the turbulent water rising steadily .

My mind drifted back to the sun-dappled hills of Mississippi. I wonder where were Poppa and Miss Fancy are right now? Do they know about this storm and are they anxious for me? And Tom, he would be frantic if he knew I was here in the midst of this charging ocean. Dear Tom. He's a regular old granny where I am concerned. I closed my eyes and silently prayed for each of my loved ones, and then prayed for safety for myself and for this family who had become so dear to me. The deep chords of my composition, "The Majesty of the Sea" came to mind, but this is not majesty. This turbulent unbridled motion, furious action and cross action, violent wind and water tears at my senses, assaults my reason, even as it batters and churns at the masonry of this man-made home they called "The Fort". Perhaps when this is all over, and I can think clearly again, I may add another movement to my composition.

Suddenly, the telephone shrilled. Henry jumped to answer it. "For you Dad."

"Hello. Is that so? Well look out for yourself. You know the safety of you men comes first. What's that? My goodness, maybe you're right. I'll see to it right away. You know I don't want you fellows to take unnecessary risks. If you think it wise, start right now and get into town. Use your own judgment and consider your safety first. What? Oh, hang the warehouses. We'll build others —we're covered by insurance. Take care of yourselves…that is what is important…look after the men! I must get busy on this end. God be with you."

"Jennings says the wind has just been reported over ninety miles an hour, and still rising, the glass is still dropping. He says the flood is terrible out there. A steamer has broken loose and is crashing around among the boats lying at anchor, threatening to smash the wharf itself. He says the wind is veering to the southeast, which means the worst is yet to come. Evidently we are caught in the vortex of the hurricane. That may produce a tidal wave. The storm whorl is moving southeast, and there is no telling what will happen if we are scooped up in that arc containing the main force of the storm. He insists that I phone for a boat and get us into town. He says it is impossible to send one out from there and reach us. All of you, hurry. Pack a bag. Put on boots and slickers. You servants also, get ready to go and I will locate a boat. Now hurry! If we are going to leave, the sooner, the better."

"Hello? Hello?… I can't get a line. Hello? Hello? Central? Is everybody in Galveston trying to telephone? Hello? Hello! Connect me with supervisor Fay Johnston. Hello, Fay, This is Hand at The Fort. Can you rustle a line for me? I've got to get my family away from here. We're like a canoe in the middle of this ocean."

"Captain Hand, I will certainly get you a connection as soon as possible. You should already be in town. The wind seems to be blowing from every direction and the flood is rushing at us from two sides. When they meet, you know what will happen to our lines?"

"They will go down, most likely, and I have to have a boat, so hurry!"

"I will do what I can. Hold on, and keep the line open. Excuse me . . . " The Captain stood listening in on the confusion in the telephone exchange. Occasionally, Miss Johnston would come in for a moment to tell him she was still trying for a line.

Suddenly, the wind began to scream with new fury. The house shook and the water took on a deeper roaring. Over the wire, he could hear renewed confusion and then screams. Dazed, he looked at the receiver. The line was dead. The sea and the bay had met in the city...And we are marooned in this puny edifice in the midst of a hurricane swept sea. There is only one hope— Fay Johnston. She might remember in the midst of all the confusion and send a boat. We might get away yet. *If* she remembers, *if* a boat can be found, and *if* it can reach us through this maelstrom. Otherwise we have no choice. We must ride out the tempest on this lonely man-made promontory. Ruefully, the Captain said, "Now it is in the hands of The Lord." The still small voice within nudged me, *"Hasn't it always been?"* Colonel Hand realized he was trembling and turned away from the phone to break the news to his anxiously waiting family. No words were necessary. His face said it all. Aunt Grace's hand flew to her mouth, and Henry reached for his sister's hand. Viney, who had been silently looking on, moved to my side and held me tightly.

Chapter 21 – Reality

After their first shock, the family took the announcement more calmly than I would have thought possible. Surely experience with other storms had given them confidence I did not feel, yet I was strengthened by their calm. The evening wore on slowly as an agony of sound continued to batter our ears. The air pressure was so heavy it was difficult to breathe. The servants went on tiptoe, but the family seldom moved. The wind crept slowly southeast, growing steadily louder and more violent. The waters rose continually, their bellowing crescendo of sound filling air and space, mingled with the pounding of the wind-tortured rain.

Aunt Grace instructed the servants, "Please serve dinner early as night will not be long coming. With the electricity gone, we would have to be served by lamplight if we wait until our usual hour. I planned a light meal. No one feels very concerned about eating." An awesome foreboding made the servants' work difficult. Dinner was quickly over, and we gathered again in the drawing room. The watch continued. Etta's petulant expression as she occasionally made trips to the window showed me her mind was still on LeJuene. Henry, who had been watching his father's face as he made frequent inspections of the water in its steady rise, suddenly sprang to his feet.

"This is worse than we thought, Father. You know it is! I can see it in your face. We can't stay here in the midst of this raging ocean. Someway, we've got to have a boat. Father, I am young and strong, and I am a good swimmer. I will swim into town and get a boat. You *must* let me!" The Captain put an arm around his son's shoulders. "It is no use son. I am proud of you for offering, but look at that water. No swimmer could survive in that sea. It is no longer just the swell that the hurricane is driving in from the south. Now the gale is pushing from west as well, so that a vicious crosscurrent and chop develops where the breakers beat on each other. The sea would quickly pound you to pieces. Even a boat would be helpless in such waters and against such wind and waves. No, there is nothing we can do now, except wait, pray God's mercy, and that the work of our hands will stand."

"But, Father . . .!" Henry began to protest, but the wise Father mutely shook his head. Henry, meeting his eyes, turned away. Watching Etta and knowing her determination had clearly been to get to LeJuene, I saw her face crumple and tears fill her eyes when she heard the resignation in her father's voice. Like one waking from a dream, she looked around at her family and at me. Slowly she registered the impact of the wind and the quaking walls. Her eyes fell on her mother and with a cry, she ran to bury her head on Aunt Grace's shoulder. She began to sob.

"There, there, my precious child. You must not be afraid of the storm. It is not to live or to die that matters, but how we face death and what we make of our lives that counts. Saint Paul said, 'For me to die is gain.' We are in the hands of our Creator and if He sees fit to take us in the midst of this storm, we can only say as our Savior did, 'Thy will be done.'" (Matthew 26:42) Quietly sobbing, Etta sat on the floor, her head on her mother's knee, her shoulders shaken by an occasional shuddering sigh. I knew it was not the storm Etta was distressed about. I thought of purifying fires, and felt that if Henrietta lived through this turmoil, she would surely grow into a fine, strong woman.

The Captain always asked a blessing at the table but tonight he offered an especially solemn and heart-felt prayer.

> "Heavenly Father, we praise you for your mighty power displayed to us daily.
> We praise you for the love you extend to us.
> Once again you are showing us your grace and mercy.
> I ask forgiveness for my sin of thinking I am strong and trusting the work of my own puny hands.
> If it be Your will, please spare us from harm in this hurricane.
> We thank you for this food and your constant provision for us.
> In the name of your son, our Savior, Jesus, we pray, Amen."

His prayer brought strength, acceptance, and a measure of peace to his family, to me, and to the servants. Night was hardly more than a deeper darkness. It came so swiftly that before the meal was finished, lamps were lit. The choppy water could be heard slapping against the floor under our feet. The whole concerto of the storm seemed to spring to new volume with the fading light.

Silently, we filed back to the drawing room. The frightened servants cleared supper away quickly and took refuge in the drawing room with the rest of us. As time dragged on, all of us became strangely quiet as together we waited wearily for the storm to pass.

Chapter 22 – Terror

Against all reasonable expectation, the tumult continued to grow ever more fearsome. The wind was a bellowing tempest. Would it never stop? The twins stood arm in arm, looking out the west window, their red hair gleaming in the flickering lamplight. Captain and Mrs. Hand and I stood near the door while Viney hovered near me, fearful and protective.

"Jes listen at dat wind," she moaned, "I aint never heard nothin like that before."

"It is bad, Viney," Captain tried to reassure us, "but I believe this house will stand against any ordinary storm wind or flood. The water is very high now, but it is still not getting into the house."

This was no ordinary storm. The raging tempest had swept up the waters of the ocean, piling them twenty feet high or more...a mountain of water rushing on toward the island. Even as we listened, a deeper howl entered into the voice of the storm. With a roar like a thousand freight trains, the monstrous wave struck the Fort. The massive oak doors were torn from their hinges and rushed in on the crest of the wave. With supercharged strength, Captain Hand seized his wife and me.

Throwing us and himself, onto one of the heavy oak doors, he locked his hands and feet to the edges of the door and held on for dear life. Instinctively imitating, Viney threw herself onto the second door and clung there like a leaf on a limb. The wind seemed alive with fury. Its irresistible force swept everything before it, water, wood, flesh, and stone. The force of the wave drove the doors with a crash, straight through the Fort's back wall, and out and away into the dark and pitching world. Faintly, I heard the grinding crash as The Fort collapsed and it's remains swept away on the rushing flood. A terrifying interval followed, compounded of motion, and sound, and heaving black water. The wind shredded our clothing, tore hair from our heads, snatched away breath and fought to tear us from that door on the churning, pitching, flood. The black air was full of rain, spray, wind and water. We hapless humans battled for breath and life. There was no thought, no speech, just roaring blackness and everlasting violent motion. Pressing instinctively, we struggled to became one with that tossing door. Eventually, our senses could stand no more and blackness deeper than night, overcame us.

Chapter 23 – Awakening

My pale skin felt as if it were on fire. The blazing sun blinded me. Blinking my eyes rapidly to try to clear them of sand and salt, I realized I could not move. Something had me pinned tightly against a rough surface. Struggling to turn my head, I saw that Captain Hand's arm was stretched across me and clasped the heavy door with an iron grip. He appeared to be dead, and I screamed desperately, "Captain Hand!" Rousing, he groaned, "Nancy, is that you? Are you all right? Where are we?" The massive hand-carved door on which we had ridden out the storm had come to rest on a huge mound of rubble. When I tried to sit up, the debris shifted precariously.

"Be still!" the captain cautioned. He edged carefully off the side of the door, climbed down, and then helped me down. Fully conscious now, he began to remember. "Grace! Retta! Henry! He shouted frantically and began to run in the direction their home had stood, desperately searching for his family. I tried to run after him, but I had lost my shoes, and I, who had never gone barefoot in my life, tripped and stumbled over broken glass, splinters and every manner of debris. I could not keep up. As far as I could see, in every direction, destruction met my eyes. I could not see a single building still standing, nor another living person. In contrast, the placid ocean lapped sleepily at the beach with the steady ebbing and flowing pulse of eternity, as if there had never been a storm.

Completely alone for the first time in my whole life, I fearfully realized I must find shelter, and clean water to quench my burning thirst and clear my eyes. I set off westward toward the central part of the island, and the city. Picking my way through or around ridges of debris, I came upon a lady's small red shoe. Picking it up, I watched as I struggled along and soon found another shoe. I laughed aloud as I put the petite red slipper on one foot and a laced a large man's brogan onto my other foot. They made walking difficult, but since I had never walked barefoot before, I was thankful for their protection. This bit of absurdity lifted my spirits a little as I picked my way down the island. Approaching a low place where the tide and heavy rains had caused the water to pool, I spotted a bright patch of color. Hurrying toward it, I realized to my horror that the bright spot was Etta's beautiful red hair swishing back and forth in the water. The twins' bodies floated in the pool, clinging to each other in death just as they had in the womb. Stricken, I began to run, stumbling, blinded by my tears.

Suddenly I heard a terrified scream and a guttural voice respond, "Shut up gal!" Then a familiar voice shouted, "Let go uv dat chile, you drunken bum!" Creeping fearfully around a mountain of debris, I saw a huge man on his knees in the sand. He grabbed the woman and threw her to the ground, choking her. Looking around frantically, I spotted a broken table leg protruding from the wreckage. I tugged it out and swung it with a strength born of desperation, striking the man across the back of his head. It knocked him out. Where he fell, beautiful jewelry spilled from his pockets—gold chains, rings and a large diamond ring still on a human finger— Struggling out from under the marauder who had fallen across her, Viney rubbed her neck, straightened her clothing, and held out her arms to me. I was terrified and sobbing hysterically.

"Viney? I thought he was going to kill you," I sobbed. "I'm so thankful to find you. Are you all right? The twins are dead and I don't know where Colonel Hand and Aunt Grace are." I was babbling uncontrollably. "Shh, hush, Nancy baby, I's okay and I'm here now and I ain't gonna let nuthin' else happen to you." Viney held me tightly in her arms, gently rocking me, back and forth, and crooning softly, as she calmed both herself and me. As we calmed, we realized a young girl, 10 or 12 years old sat on the sand nearby. Her clothes were almost torn off. She was hugging them to her, trembling and sobbing softly. Quickly, Viney pulled the child into her arms, comforting her.

"It's okay, Honey. That monster ain't gonna bother you no more, either. What's yo' name chile?" "E . . E. . . Elizabeth," she gasped. Taking me by one hand and Elizabeth by the other, Viney led us rapidly away. "Come on chillun, we best git ourselves as far away from that drunken bum as we kin." Turning to me, she explained,

"He had dis po chile down, an wuz ripping her clothes when I heard her scream and ran to hep her."

Hurrying down the beach, Viney led us to a makeshift shelter she had discovered earlier. A fallen piece of a roof, supported by some crossed beams had created a sort of cave one could crawl into. Before setting out to find me, Viney had stocked her shelter from a wrecked grocery store. There were no labels on any of the cans, but all had liquid in them to quench our thirst while the food provided nourishment. The corner of a broken brick made do as a can opener. Though canned milk, peaches, corn, and sauerkraut seemed a strange meal when retold later, it made a feast for us hungry survivors.

Chapter 24 – In Mississippi

September 8, 1900

Tom Huggins woke before daylight from a dream about Nancy. In the dream, a terrible roaring prevented him from reaching her. Around him the quiet sounds of a peaceful Mississippi night slowly dispelled the roaring from his conscious mind. The chirping of cicada and cricket, a burst of song as a mocking bird sang in the night, croaking of frogs in the slough, the deep "ker-chunk" of a bullfrog down by the lake—To one attuned to hearing, the Mississippi night is alive with sound. Tom both heard and loved it, but the disturbance of the dream remained and he could not get back to sleep. He rose in the grey pre-dawn and walked under the dark oaks of his homestead. He wandered to the lot fence where he leaned on his arms and gazed at his horses, Tem and Sunshine. He had done this often since Nancy went away, for somehow he felt closer to her in the presence of these horses on which they had ridden so many happy hours. It was she who had named them "Tempest and Sunshine" because of contrast in color rather than disposition. Tem was a gleaming black, with a white blaze on his forehead. His luxuriant mane, tail and smooth sides shone with the sheen of black satin. Sunshine was a delicate palomino with blond mane and tail. Some connoisseurs considered palominos the most beautiful of horses. He never let anyone else ride Sunshine. He was grooming a colt of the same perfection so that when they married, and Nancy came as mistress of Blue Haven, she might have the matched pair for her buggy-team.

Tom's plantation, Blue Haven, was so named because it was approached through a screen of venerable live oaks and pecan trees. Beyond the trees one skirted a spring fed lake as blue as the summer sky. When emerging from the shade of the ancient trees, the intense brilliance of the Mississippi sky reflected in the slightly darker blue of the water. Then across the lake, the fine architecture and beautiful symmetry of house and grounds came into view. Tonight, Tom did not feel comforted, even when Tempest whinnied gently and pushed his soft muzzle against Tom's arm. Sunshine stood nearby, her dainty ears pricked forward, her gentle eyes regarding him intently. He could not seem to bring Nancy near to him in thought even with these companions of their happy times. He watched the landscape lighten as a pink and gold haze began to color the clouds and reflect in the calm lake. A rooster crowed, birds started their day-long twitter. A symphony of colors wrote themselves across lake and sky. This morning, however, it held small interest for Tom. As the sun came up full and bright, he resolved to ride over to Silver Lake as soon as he had breakfasted, for a visit with the Norsworthys. This decision released some of his tension. He smiled grimly.

"You're in a bad way Tom, when just the thought of her

parents can comfort you." But he had never made any pretense about his devotion to Nancy.

* * * *

Malinda, the Norsworthy's housekeeper, answered his knock. "Good morning, Marse Tom. Come right on in. De folks is havin' coffee. Jes go right on in and join 'em." Tom entered the dining room, and the Colonel stood, "Good morning, Tom. It is so nice to see you. We have missed you since Nancy's been away."

"I have missed coming over, I assure you." Tom smiled, shook hands with his future father-in-law and kissed Mrs. Norsworthy on her cheek. "I hope Nancy will be back soon so I will have an excuse to hang around again as usual."

"Now Tom, you know no excuse is needed. You are always welcome." At that moment there was a knock at the door and Mr. Lofton came in with some newspapers under his arm.

"Good morning Mrs. Norsworthy, Sam. How are you, Tom? While I was in town, I bought some newspapers. Each of the papers has news about a hurricane that ran off the beaten track and contrary to usual, is traveling westward in the Gulf of Mexico. It promises to do a great deal of damage where it hits the coast. We looked in the atlas and Galveston is right where the coast begins to bend. Of course it may hit further south, and we hope it does, but since Nancy is down there, I thought you would like to know about the storm. Everybody in town is talking about it. Here are the papers."

"Thank you John. We appreciate you thinking of us." Suddenly Colonel Norsworthy spoke to the servant pouring coffee for Tom,

"What's that Malindy? Why are you muttering to yourself? Speak up!"

"Taint nuthin, Marse Norsworthy. Jes—several of the Black people been having bad dreams. They skeered sompin gonna happen to Miss Nancy."

"Nonsense, Malindy!" The Colonel spoke sharply. "You shouldn't say such things and upset your mistress."

"Well sir, I tole you it 'twant nothin', but you ast me."

"Let's not have any more of that nonsense. Clear these things away." As he intended, the exodus from the table created a diversion, but the harm had been done, for Southerners were familiar with the Negroe's uncanny penchant for dreams. In fact, some of them seemed to possess a talent for premonition and intuition. As soon as possible, Tom excused himself, and the Colonel walked him out to his horse.

"I wouldn't say anything inside sir, not wishing to add to Mrs. Norsworthy's distress, but I have been worried about Nancy myself. That is really why I came over this morning. If she hadn't made me promise not to come down there, I would leave here this morning.

"Sometimes promises have to be broken, my boy. No one could have foreseen these circumstances. Her mother and I would rest easier if we knew you were with her."

"Do you really think the circumstances justify it sir? Nancy is so proud. I would hate to upset her." Nancy's father smiled ruefully. "I think she might forgive you. But you know, you would arrive only after the storm had passed."

"That's true, but unless I am mistaken, there is a train that leaves Meridian at 10:30 a.m. If I take a short cut I know of through the woods and ride hard, I can make it. I'll be on my way at once."

"That is impossible, Tom. You would kill your horse!"

"I would do it if necessary, sir, but I am wasting precious time.

"You're taking a long chance my boy, but God bless you. Take care of our girl and give her our love. We will be praying for your safety as well as hers."

Chapter 25 – Determination

Incredibly, Tom made the train connection and began a journey fraught with high water, disrupted connections, and determination. Arriving two days later, six miles from Galveston Bay, the train could go no further. For hours they had ridden through country that gave evidence of the storm. The scene at the end of the of the rail service defied reason. The prairie was strewn with incredible wreckage. Human bodies were indiscriminately mixed with debris. The sight struck horror in Tom. Consciously he wanted to rush about the prairie viewing each body with the awful query, "Is it Nancy?"

Driven by his better judgment, he felt compelled to get to Galveston, so, with several others, he set out on foot. He walked for what seemed hours, before he spotted a forlorn looking horse grazing in the slime-covered grass. He spoke gently to the animal, grasped its mane and mounted. Without saddle or bridle, Tom turned the horse toward the island. In the distance, he could see a huge bulk. As he moved nearer, logic told him what his eyes observed was impossible. But there it sat. A huge steamship of enormous length sat in the field, miles from any body of water. He asked himself, *what monstrous action of nature could have moved this Leviathan of the deep so far from its native habitat? And what of an island only a few feet above sea level which lay in its path?* His anxiety for Nancy grew. He drove the horse into a trot and urged it toward the bay. Soggy marshes and the broken remains of the road made difficult passage.

Finally arriving at the shore, Tom found himself facing a vast stretch of water filled with wreckage of every description. The two mile long bridge was completely destroyed. He had struggled to get this far only to meet another obstacle. He groaned in frustration, but said aloud, "I will not quit now." Quickly, he undressed. Laying his coat on the ground, he piled his shoes and other garments methodically on it, making a pack, which he fastened on his back using belt and suspenders.

With determination born of desperation, Tom plunged into the bay. He swam to the first pier of the wrecked bridge, clung to it, rested, and swam again. His weary actions became automatic... swim and rest... swim and rest. Night came and still he made his way from pier to pier, resting at each, then struggling to the next. He was barely conscious when his feet finally struck the sandy bottom and he could scramble out onto the shore. Dragging himself up on the beach, he fell sprawling and slept until he felt the burning rays of the sun on his back. Moving stiffly, Tom pulled on his shoes and sodden garments and made his way toward the wrecked city.

Borne on the gulf breeze, a vile odor assaulted his nostrils. As he drew near the city, the odor became stronger and more repulsive—the aroma of death, destruction, and all things soaked in sea water and steamed in the sun. The island presented a picture of absolute desolation. Wreckage, strewn and twisted, was interwoven everywhere with bodies, swollen and festering. As he passed, Tom gazed fearfully, always with the question in his mind, "Is Nancy one of those?' Yet, under a compulsion he could not fathom, he pushed on. He came to a section of the city where the streets were partially cleared. Perhaps here he could find someone to aid him in his search. Dully, he perceived gangs of men loading corpses onto wagons. Seeing a man with a gun who seemed to be in charge of the laborers, Tom approached him.

"Excuse me sir, but could you tell me how anyone would locate a visitor in this city?

"What in tarnation do you mean, 'locate a visitor? Bud, the angel Gabriel don't know where nobody is in this city. Just look at 'em, rich and poor, black and white, all of 'em dead, 95% of 'em naked, and don't *nobody know who* they are. Nothin' to do but burn 'em, all alike. We tried burying 'em, there was just too many. Tried takin' 'em out to sea, but the tide brought 'em back, all black and bloated... busting wide open on the beach. It's just impossible. All we can do is burn 'em, and nobody wants to help...Locate somebody? Who on earth do you think you are, a magician? ...Where did you come from anyway?"

"I'm Tom Huggins from Mississippi and I'm trying to locate a young lady who was visiting the Hands of Hand & Co. Importers and Exporters."

"Well 'Sir Galahad,' Hand *was* a big shot once, but they all look alike when they get like that." He flipped a hand at the awful cargo on the wagon. "How did you get here, anyway?"

"I swam the bay."

"Swam the bay? You're quite a liar, I'll give ya that! Ain't no one could do that even in a normal tide. Huh, likely story, Mr. Huggins, but I'm glad you're here. Yes sir, I'm *very glad* you're here. Loading these dead folks is a job needs lots of hands and yours is as good as any so *get busy!*"

"I'm sorry fellow, but I came to this city to find Miss Norsworthy and if possible to get her back home to her folks, and that has to be my first job."

"Sorry?" The man guffawed. "Everybody's sorry. Everybody's looking for somebody. And, *nobody* wants to handle these dead folks, so they're rottin' all over the streets and we're all gonna die of the plague lessen somebody cleans up this mess. So..." the man with the gun laughed raucously,

"We Ain't Askin.' We're Tellen'! Now you fall in there an' lend a hand before I shoot you down and burn you with the rest of 'em. Get Busy!" As Tom protested the man advanced on him with gun drawn and a hard gleam in his eye.

Some of the others called out, "Come on. You ain't no better than the rest of us!" When Tom took hold of a swollen body and felt the putrid flesh in his hands, the awful odor, he turned and was violently ill.

"Come on you!" bawled the man with the gun. "Sure you're sick. We all are! But that don't get the job done. Load 'em up!"

"Hey, get back from there, Lady. I don't care if he is your husband. They all got to go alike! It's the livin' we got to think about... Get that wagon on outta here and bring up another'n. We got to keep 'em movin'.'"

Dazed, Tom fell in and worked at the gruesome task. As he worked, one thought haunted him, seeing the dead bodies piled on the wagons, viewing each face, *"Is Nancy among this sad freight or is she somewhere helpless and I can't get to her?"* He became tired past fatigue, revolted, and helpless. He tore off part of his shirt, tied it over his nose, and labored automatically. Thoughts of Nancy kept him going. *How will I find you? I've got to get away from here, but how? Nancy, are you safe?"*

"Lord Jesus, please hold Nancy close in your protective hand."

139

Liquor passed among them. Tom would not drink it; but he poured it over him, from head to foot—especially his hands. He looked at his hands and wondered if they would ever be clean again. Around midnight, Tom was finally able to slip away from this terrible task.

Chapter 26 – Survival

In the broken roof cave, the fiercely hot and grueling hours crept by. I slept the sleep of exhaustion with my head in Viney's lap. The young girl we had rescued, Elizabeth, snuggled tight against Viney's leg. Though hot and exhausted herself, with only the broken table leg for a weapon, Viney struggled to stay awake in the pitch dark. She would protect her charges against any of the drunken looters and marauders prowling in the night. Finally, dawn broke. Gently stroking Nancy's salt stiff hair, Viney urged, "Nancy, baby, I kinda hate to leave this safe place, but we gotta find Mistuh Hand if we can, and see 'bout gettin' outa here and back home to yo Momma and Poppa."

We each had one last can of mystery food for moisture and nourishment, but with hunger and thirst still tormenting us, we crawled out of the dubious shelter of our cave. Viney insisted on taking with us our only weapon—the old table leg. Outside, I gasped at the confusion. The brilliant sun almost blinded us.

"Where are the streets? There are huge barriers—twisted trees mixed with broken wires, poles and bricks, wood and all kinds of broken things everywhere. How will we ever get through?" Viney answered patiently, "Jes like we always do anything, Sweet Chile, one step at the time. With God's help, we'll take one step at the time, together." Climbing cautiously, and picking our way, we made slow progress toward where the city should be. Everywhere there were lifeless bodies, and vacant-faced people searching endlessly for their missing family members. Ahead of us staggered a bowlegged old man, drunk and still drinking from a bottle clutched in one hand. His faded clothing spoke of poverty, but his pockets, even under the edges of his hat, and his hatband bulged with money—sodden, but unmistakable hundreds of bills.

We saw two men lift a rooftop where it had landed on the juncture of two fallen walls. When they raised it, one wall fell outward and revealed the figure of a well-dressed man on his knees, his face lifted and his hands clasped in prayer. I gasped. Viney shook her head.

"Drowned on his knees!" one of the men said.

"It's dat LeJuene. He *did* think of the hereafter, after all." Viney urged me onward and I responded numbly. "Walk in the edge uv the water, chile. It'll cool yo feet." On the beach, I stumbled over a tree limb and fell down.

"I just can't go any further." I crumpled on the sand—crying. Viney took me by the arm and urged me to get up saying firmly, "One day, you gone be perfect. Sweet Jesus gonna put roun' you a robe uv richusness, take yo hand an lead you to the great God uv the whole universe. You wont never be tired again, You'll fall on yo knees, and sing wid the angels gathered roun' the great white throne in heaven, but dis—ain't—dat—day. Today, He'll hep you take one step at a time. Come on now, pick yo self up an' take a step. De Lawd, He say lay aside every weight and run da race set befoe us. De Lawd be our strength.

(Hebrews 12:1 and Philipians 4:13. Viney's interpretation.) It can't be too much fudder. We can't stay here—aint safe. You 'member that Psalm 23? Take a deep breath an say it with me."

"The Lawd is my shepherd."

He done saved us from the storm. He gone hep us home. He with us *now*.

"Come on, say it:"

"Come on Baby, now say it. I lifted my head and began, as had multitudes before me, to draw strength from the beloved promises.

"The Lord is my shepherd, I shall not want.
He makes me lie down in green pastures.
He leads me beside still waters,
He restores my soul"

"A-men...Praise de Lawd, He really do!"

"He guides me in paths of righteousness for His name's sake.
Even though I walk through the valley of the shadow of death..."

"Lawd have Mercy, we is in it."

"I will fear no evil for you are with me."

"Your rod and your staff they comfort me."

Because we were all deadly weary, a sudden attack of "exhaustion silly giggles" came over us as Viney raised her "staff"...the old table leg...which she had been using as a walking stick. Hysterical laughter echoed back and forth between us. Even Elizabeth joined in. Finally, we pulled ourselves together and Viney pleaded,

"Please, God, forgive us. We didn't mean no disrespect."

"We gotta keep movin', Chillun. Keep movin' one step, den anudder." Slowly we made progress toward where the town should be. Nothing looked familiar. *Has any of the city survived?*

The day was almost spent, and so were we, when Viney heard a questioning shout,

"*Viney!* Is that really you?"

"Mista Tom! *That really IS You!*" Grabbing him and wrapping him in a bear hug, she danced him around and around shouting, "Hallelooya! Thank you Lawd! Praise de Lawd.! Thank you Lawd! You has sent yo Angel uv mercy to rescue us! Hallelooya!" Tears of joy and relief traced riverlets down her sandy, salty face. I turned to look. Exhausted and in shock, I squinted my eyes and stared blankly at my beloved Tom . . . not believing what I was seeing. Tom stared at the pitiful figure before him. He fell to his knees and stretched out his arms to me.

"Oh, my precious Nancy. You are alive!" I stood there mouth agape, dirty, sunburned, with matted hair, shredded garments and those ridiculous shoes, but Tom fell to his knees, stretched out his arms to me and said, "Oh my darling Nancy, what a beautiful sight you are. You have never been more beautiful to me, my beloved."

"I Praise you, Merciful God, my Nancy is alive." Embracing me tenderly, he sobbed,

"Thank you, Lord Jesus, for protecting Nancy and Viney, these precious children of yours."

Still not sure that my senses were not playing tricks, I collapsed into Tom's loving arms. Cradling me gently, he tenderly kissed my swollen, cracked lips. Ever so softly, he kissed the tears from my inflamed, sandy eyes. When I had recovered sufficiently from my shock, Tom carefully supported me with one arm, and Viney, clinging to Elizabeth's hand with the other as he led our exhausted trio toward the setting sun, where we hoped to find whatever remained of the city.

Chapter 27 – Rescue

I woke in a clean, comfortable bed, Viney standing beside me. There was a terrible odor in the air. "Viney? What is that? I have never smelled anything like it."

"Of course you never. Baby you slept so long you got to come to gradul. Do you 'member we is in Galveston?" Before I could answer, I gagged. A lady whom I did not know stepped forward and offered a little cheesecloth bag filled with dried herbs. She tied it over tied it over my nose.

"There …that's better isn't it?" Indeed it was a little better. I never did remember how we got from the "cave" to the Masonic Building. Here, there was a constant flow of busyness and murmuring as the men came and went. The women tore any fabric they could find into strips to be used as bandages. As they worked, they talked.

"In some places, wreckage is forty feet high…"

"And the bodies…May God forgive me, it's awful! We tried at first to establish a morgue. John Sealy and Vaughn Monroe and a couple of other men started to lay them out, but they overflowed the tables, the counters, the beds, and finally even the floors. It was necessary to start burying them, unidentified, and still they came faster than we could manage. Horrible..."

"Now, every thirty feet there is a bonfire. Dozens of them." She shook her head.

"You never saw anything like it. Bodies caught in even the tallest trees!"

"Martial law is being set up ."

"I saw a building today that was still standing, but the metal roof was rolled up like a napkin stuck in a ring."

"Over in the east part of town, the men heard a dog barking frantically. They made their way to him and found him scratching at a fallen building. Some workers got a hold of the roof, lifted it and under it were three sleeping children. The men thought at first they were dead, but they opened their eyes. None of them even have a scratch."

There was a stir at the door. A doctor entered, and close behind him two men carried a limp form. "Put him over here," said the doctor wearily, as he prepared to administer a hypodermic. "This man was working with a loading gang. He picked up the putrid forms of two children. He pitched them onto the wagon and toppled in a dead faint."

"They were his own," said one of the men who had helped bring him in.

"Did you hear about the woman who located her house and righted an overturned dressing table. When she opened a drawer, a prairie dog hopped out of it? Scared the daylights outta her."

"No, I hadn't heard that one," a quiet voice spoke up. "But I'll tell you what happened to me. I remembered the importance my mother placed on some papers in her possession. She had told us they were in a wall safe behind a certain picture. They were supposed to be proof of our succession to an estate in England, and the title that went with it. After the storm, I made my way back into the house and managed to get to the picture. As I raised my hand to move it, a water moccasin reared up behind it and struck at me. Being on edge anyway, I ran, and you can believe it or not, I had no more than cleared the porch when the entire house fell down and drifted away on the water. If it had not been for that snake, I would have been in the house when it collapsed."

"My goodness! I guess those papers are gone forever now." At one table people were making crude flags, just pieces of cloth tied to rough sticks.

"What are those for? May I help?"

"Those are 'Sad Flags,' they are used as markers to show workers where bodies are to be found." I sat down, and began to tear strips of cloth. About that time another group of weary men arrived. They accepted coffee and dropped into chairs, continuing the conversation.

"You never saw anything like it. Some of us couldn't understand the arrival of bleached bones on the beach. Those bloated bodies…yes, but bones? Well can you believe it? The very soil of the graveyard had given up its dead."

"So many poor souls," said one man. "Pitched right into eternity. No way to identify them…many will never be identified."

An older man of medium height, clad in a strange mixture of clothing came in. He wore a weary, sad expression on his face, but there was something almost regal in his bearing.

"Captain Hand!" I shouted, and rushed across the room into his arms, almost knocking him off his feet. He looked surprised, then with a glimpse of Viney, comprehension dawned. His questioning gaze touched my hair, swung back to Viney, and his arm tightened about me.

"Nancy! Thank God you are safe. When I left you I was barely conscious and after burying my family, I searched and searched for you, but couldn't find you."

"Then you did find the twins, and were able to bury them… Aunt Grace also? Oh, I'm so sorry for your terrible loss."

"Yes. But I thank God, they are not in that awful cargo, or in those flickering fires on the beach." He touched my strange silver white hair, and his eyes questioned Viney. She just shook her head. I had not seen a mirror, yet, and was unaware of the change.

"That happened near over night, Mista Hand. But she's awright, thank God. Now ifen I kin jes get her home to her Momma and Poppa."

By Thursday, the stench was unbearable. Confusion, weariness, thirst, and hunger prevailed. The worst problem was lack of clean water. Samuel Taylor Coleridge expressed it well in *The Rime of the Ancient Mariner*. "Water, water everywhere and not a drop to drink." On this island surrounded by the lapping ocean, there was no fresh water to be found anywhere. Tongues were swollen, lips cracked. Suddenly, the parching sun seemed to hide. All faces turned skyward as rain came pouring down. Though a few grumbled, "Just what we need . . . rain. It'll soak all this mess and make it really impossible," but most rejoiced! Someone shouted, "Just think people, our prayers are being answered! Rain is fresh water!" Soon the island was in a flurry. People grabbed anything that would hold water. And as rain came pouring down, people lifted their heads, moistened their parched lips and washed filthy hands and faces. They held their vessels aloft, danced, and laughed gratefully.

During the excitement over fresh water, Captain Hand entered the Masonic Building quietly. He whispered something to me and motioned to Tom. There was a moment of quiet discussion, and I beckoned to Viney and Elizabeth.

"We are going for a walk," he said softly. Outside, I protested, "But Captain Hand, I hate to run off without saying a word. There is so much work to do and they've been so nice to me." "I know, Nancy, but sometimes discretion is the better part of wisdom. Trust me. If it were known that I have a boat leaving, it would literally be swamped with people who want to get off this island. It is only because I am in the shipping business that I can get you out of here. Your parents must be frantic, and I don't want you to miss this chance."

Comprehension dawned and we eagerly agreed. This time, none of us had any baggage to worry about. We hurried along, passing work groups, sad flags, wandering, searching people, and saddest of all, children roaming, intently seeking familiar faces. Soon we saw a tall, kind faced man, with children all around him.

"That man is Mr. Buckner, from the Baptist Orphanage in Dallas. God bless Him."

As we moved away from the center of town, our progress became more difficult. The odor in this untouched section was horrible beyond belief. The little nosebags were not enough now. Viney, Elizabeth and I covered our noses with our arms, as well. Finally Captain Hand led us into a barely passable section of a street. He hurried us down it as rapidly as possible. At the end of the path, he had concealed a small tender from a private yacht, tied to a fallen beam. Tom quickly agreed to row. The Captain apologized for the inconvenience, but laughing aloud, Tom assured him this passage would certainly be easier than his trip over *from* the mainland had been.

We quickly loaded into the small boat, and with a shove of his foot, the Captain launched us, three Mississippians and Elizabeth, out upon the wreckage-cluttered bay. Though I had hugged Captain Hand tightly and through my tears thanked him sincerely, I did not look back.

Chapter 28 – Going Home

Tom's strong arms grew very tired rowing all the way across the bay, but his grateful spirit, to be taking us safely home, kept him rowing. When we finally felt the boat drag on the sandy bottom, he rolled up his pant legs, jumped in, and pulled and pushed the loaded boat onto the Texas beach. Though the desolation gave evidence of the storm, as far as we could see, it was not impassable. Thanks to the assistance of the fine workers at the rescue station, we women had acquired serviceable shoes and once on dry land, we cheerfully began walking. We had not walked far, when Tom observed a scruffy looking man, with an equally scruffy looking horse and wagon, scavenging for usable items in the storm debris. For a generous fee, the man was happy to unload his wagon on the spot and take us several miles to the end of the train line.

"Sir," I gratefully told him, "You are an angel in disguise." A huge smile, broke out on his decrepit face, revealing several missing teeth.

As I had so many times in these last miserable days, I silently "counted my blessings," and a question flashed into my mind, *I wonder how long it has been since anyone has spoken kindly to this man?* Impulsively, I turned back long enough to give him a quick hug and thanked him again for his kind help. From the corner of my eye, I saw him wipe a tear onto his dirty, ragged sleeve.

On the train, I turned to Tom and gently kissed his hand, blistered from the long hours rowing, and whispered to him, "What do you think of a wedding on Christmas day?" He pretended to consider. "Hmm—I don't think that is a good idea—How about Thanksgiving?" And right there on the train, he pulled me to him and kissed me in front of all those strangers!

From the seat behind us, (Tom had insisted that Viney be allowed to ride with us as my nurse assistant, rather than in the car assigned to black people,) I heard her chuckle and say, "Praise de Lawd. He done used duh storm to wash some sense into dat head a yors," She stood, and stretched over the seat back to kiss the top of my head. When we finally arrived home we slept most of three days, waking just long to soak in a blessed warm bath, eat a little and sleep again. Viney wanted nothing more than "to get back to my reglar rounds."

Chapter 29 – Reflections

My grandmother, Miss Becky, always said, "Some life changes creep upon us like playful kittens. Others pounce on us like roaring lions." I guess I have experienced both kinds of changes this year. Perhaps it took both kinds for me to recognize how blessed I am, and to be ready to take responsibility for being a good steward of God's great Grace to me.

On Thanksgiving Day, 1900, I became Mrs. Thomas Elijah Huggins. The beloved Clear Creek Church was too small to hold all the guests, so we held our wedding in the nearby County Courthouse. The courtroom was beautifully decorated with colorful sprays of fall leaves, goldenrod, and other wild flowers tied with deep green ribbons. I was grateful to wear the beautiful ivory silk wedding dress worn by my grandmother and my mother before me. I silently prayed that I would be as much a blessing to my beloved Tom, as they had each been to their dear husbands. My attendants wore gowns made of amber colored taffeta Poppa had ordered from Jackson and had specially delivered to our home to be made into their gowns. I confess to being biased, but I thought our wedding was the most beautiful one I had ever seen. My best friend, Sally stood as my maid of honor. Cousin Florence, Anjelica and young Elizabeth were bridesmaids.

Remembering our joking about bitter weeds on that day last summer, Sally sneaked some golden bitterweed blooms into my wedding bouquet of lovely wildflowers. They were the perfect complement to the beautiful daisies and blackeyed susans.

"See, she told me, bitterweeds do have a purpose besides making the milk taste bitter if the cows eat them." *Yes, I silently thought, and they could also symbolize the bitter side of my fun and adventures in Galveston. Oh, how I wished Aunt Grace, Etta and Henry could have been here with Captain Hand to help us celebrate this blessed occasion. I know they are with Jesus in heaven, but I miss them and will always be thankful for the privilege of knowing them.*

After Mrs. Lofton played the wedding march on the pump organ, which had been moved here for the wedding. I stepped into the room and sang to Tom, a song I had written especially for this time. I chose the words from the Biblical book of Ruth. chapter 1:16.

My voice had finally become crystal clear again after nearly losing it from the after-effects of the hurricane. I sang

> *"Entreat me not to leave thee*
> *Nor to return from following after thee.*
> *For where thou goest I will go*
> *And where thou lodgest I will lodge.*
> *Thy people will be my people*
> *And thy God, my God."*
> *I will honor thee, and I will cherish thee.*
> *I will sing praise to our God for thee,*
> *All the days of our lives.*

My proud Poppa walked me down the aisle, and after our pastor lead us in our vows to each other, and prayed for each of us and for our permanent union, he finally pronounced us married! The reception was held in the rotunda of the courthouse. A multitude of guests came through our greeting line. Cora, our long time cook, had created a beautiful three-tiered cake. We served it with Viney's delicious fruit punch. No alcohol would be served at our wedding. A chamber ensemble provided music for dancing. Toward the end of the evening, Tom surprised and delighted me with a country jig, prearranged with the musicians. We whirled and kicked up our heels in joyful fun, just I had wished we could do at the governor's ball at Rosemont last summer. Our wedding celebration was long remembered around the community, as "delightfully different."

Perhaps that delightful difference was a foreshadowing of things to come. Our lives were anything but dull. On the next Thanksgiving Day, I gave birth to husky twin sons. We named them Daniel Elijah and Thomas Samuel, but they were soon called Tommy and Danny. Their proud grandpoppa planted two magnolia trees at Blue Haven to grow and honor the boys as they grew. At my request, Viney was seated in a comfortable chair in my room. The happy father of the twins, Tom, the newly elected Governor of Mississippi, placed Danny in one of Viney's arms and Tommy in her other arm. Tears came to her eyes as she remembered when I, her "Nancy Baby", had first been placed in her arms twenty years ago. Gathering her strength of purpose, she prayed,

Thank you, Lawd Jesus, for sendin' these two lil' cherubs to bless Mista Tom and my Nancy Baby. Thank you for lettin' us sometimes hol' angels 'thout even knowin' we are doin' it. Thank you Lawd Jesus for lovin' us so good! Aaa-men!"

On Christmas Day, 1901, beloved Viney was laid to her eternal rest under the trees in the Norsworthy family cemetery at Silver Lake. She had never fully recovered from the debilitating effects of the hurricane and its aftermath. When she contracted influenza, early in December, She would not rest, nor allow anyone to take care of her. She declared emphatically,

"I wuz born to serve, like Jesus. 'He say "I came to serve, not to be served."(Mathew 20:28) I wuz born a slave. When I wuz freed, I chose to be a free servant. I done serve my family here all my life. I don't know how to *be* served. I be too old to change now. I wanta serve my Nancy an' her family here 'till I go to serve Jesus."

Viney had been my mother's playmate when they were children. When I was born, she asked to be my Mammy. I had never known life without her. My dear friend who served me from her heart will be sorely missed.

On April 29, 1903 Rebecca Violet Sue Huggins came into our family. She quickly charmed her devoted brothers, and as she grew, it became clear she had inherited her mother's musical talent. In clear, perfect pitch, she sang to the family dog, the horses, roses and whatever else attracted her attention. She was a tiny golden haired sprite, named for a beloved servant. (Violet was Viney's correct name, but it had evolved to Viney in my baby speech). Our daughter was dubbed "Susie" by her adoring brothers. She thought she could do anything her brothers could do and the trio got into mischief together frequently. Susie loved and charmed all creatures great and small.

Tom and I delighted in our children, who could be found singing and playing around Rosemont, or the capitol building, always with a parent close by. They were taught good manners, proper decorum, and carefully schooled in academics, but we allowed each to develop his, or her, own individual personality and interests.

Governor Tom and I never forgot how helpless we had felt in the aftermath of the storm, and how readily people from so many walks of life had helped us. We were privileged, through his office, to bring about many reforms in education, healthcare, broader economic opportunities,and other changes which benefitted families, women, and children in our chosen state, Mississippi.

Chapter 30 – Maturity

1905 in Central Mississippi

On a hard-packed sand-clay road out of Jackson, Mississippi, an arresting sight flashed past two hunters, just emerging from the scrub oak woods. They carried their guns down by their sides and their coats bulged with game. A buggy and team was not an unusual sight in this country...not even a two-seater like this one with its black paint and red wheels gleaming. The beauty and grace of the matched team *was* unusual. Not only were they palominos, their blond manes and tails streaming out in graceful curves, but there was in their movements a certain joy, as if fully conscious of their perfect performance. On the back seat sat three beautiful children, reveling in the swift motion. But the most arresting sight was the beauty and grace of the driver, a silver haired young lady, sitting erect and balanced as a butterfly. The horses' gait was so swift as to verge upon run-away, yet everything seemed under perfect control. In a mere moment, they had flashed by and were receding down the road, leaving behind them a flash of their own high spirits reflected in the hunters' faces.

"Who was that, for goodness sake?"

"Don't tell me you have never seen Governor Huggins' family."

"Was *that* Mrs. Huggins? What a beauty. That whole outfit was like something out of a painting—too perfect to be real." His companion laughed. "Are you speaking of the driver or the horses?"

"Both, if I may be so bold. But say—isn't it dangerous to drive that fast? With the slightest acceleration those horses would have been running away."

Not that pair and not with that driver. Wilder horses than that behave with her hands on the reins. Those palominos were raised by hand and trained by Tom Huggins for her personal use. They understand her perfectly. That swift pace is an expression of mutual delight. The neighbors swear that team can smile!"

"Well I don't know about that, but they certainly seem to fly. I don't think I would want to travel that fast in a buggy."

"Well, to be honest, I wouldn't either. But I probably wouldn't feel that way, if I was the kind of a driver Nancy Huggins is."

"So, its first names, huh? Well, I shall expect you to introduce me tonight at the Governor's ball. That was quite a sight, but say—I knew there was something unusual! Did you notice her hair?" He turned a puzzled face to his fellow hunter.

"Oh yes, I have seen her many times. She was in Galveston at the time of the 1900 hurricane. The experiences she had there caused her hair to turn the color of new silver."

"Really? Did it change her any other way?"

"Well, she is serious about really serious things, but otherwise I have seldom seen anyone with the joy of living she displays."

"The Governor must be one lucky guy. I look forward to meeting them both."

"You will have that opportunity tonight at the Governor's Ball and you will find them both just as charming as you are anticipating."